To Save A Life

Stunts performed by Sean Bolton

Published by

Langhorne Creative Group

Nashville, Tennessee

Get more information about this and other Langhorne titles by liking us on Facebook and visiting us at langhornecreativegroup.com. For a brief history of Byzantium and why you should give a damn, check out the Introduction to Byzantium section at the back of the book.

The story you are about to read is, tragically, based on real history: graphic, bloody history. Please don't let your kids read this.

For Lord John Julius Norwich, for showing me the closest Heaven ever came to Earth.

For my love, without whom my life and this work would be without merit.

Introduction

The story you are about to read is true to history, but this is not a history book. The story of the Eastern Roman Empire, most commonly known as Byzantium, started in the founding of the Roman Empire by Julius Caesar, perhaps the most influential man in history besides Jesus Christ. As the original city of Rome grew in power and influence through the centuries, it fed the lusts of its people on the blood, flesh, and wealth of their neighbors, some innocent, some not. It was a pagan, brutal empire, but it spread over half of Europe, all of North Africa, and most of the Middle East, with Iraq forming the conflict zone between Rome and the fierce might of Persia, Rome's great rival for world empire.

In 313 AD, however, the Roman Emperor Constantine the Great changed the inhuman brutality that had provided pagan Rome its soul. He adopted the Christian faith and founded a new capitol for a Christian Roman Empire in Constantinople, known today as Istanbul. As the meeting place between Europe and Asia, this seat of the eastern part of the Roman Empire would live on for 1,000 years after the West was lost to the barbarian hordes. It kept the light of civilization burning, and in a cataclysmic war that wrecked both empires, the Eastern Roman Emperor Heraclius smashed the Persian Empire once and for all.

At that moment, the Islamic invasion of the outside world began, with the Persians consumed and the Romans fighting for their very existence. The rock of Constantine's City held, and Europe was spared the conquest of Islam for a time. The history of the Eastern Empire would continue on as an unrelenting war between Constantinople, with its love of Christianity, artistry, and learning, and the Muslim east, with its love of slavery and submission.

After centuries of different fates, the Christians of the East and the West grew apart, their leadership fought one another over spiritual niceties, and hostility blossomed between the two Christendoms. But even in the face of sometimes bloody bickering, when Emperor Alexius Comnenus asked the Pope for money and mercenaries to help him fight the Muslim Turks, a fierce nomadic people who relentlessly raided his Empire, the Pope responded with vigor to aid his Eastern brethren by launching the Crusades. The unruly mob of knights and peasants running amok in his Empire was not what the Emperor had wanted, but the first three Crusades succeeded in buying the Empire breathing room from his unending wars with the Turks. The price was great, though, as the help sent from the Catholic West was rapacious and self-serving, and the Crusaders who risked their lives in defense of the Empire thought the Byzantines to be faithless traitors. The two Christendoms drifted ever more dangerously apart.

While Byzantium eventually fell to the Turks in 1453, leaving Eastern Europe open to centuries of oppression and terror, it was the Fourth Crusade that destroyed the heart of the Empire. When the sultan entered Constantinople, he was simply closing a ledger ruined by Catholic violence. This book tells the story of the Fourth Crusade, both of those who struggled to save the Christian Roman Empire and those who sought to destroy it. This is the tale of those men in their time and the choices they made. This is the tale of the ending of an age, and we live with the consequences of that cataclysm to this day.

To Save A Life

Constantinople, July 25th, 1261

The bitter wind made him clutch his cloak ever closer to his body, lest he die of the elements. Not that it mattered anymore. To him, anyway.

The waning moon hung far off in the sky, on a night where no stars shone. Its cold light cast great shadows, ultimately doing more to shine out the darkness than bring forth the light. Were there any to see it, the watcher cast barely a silhouette.

There was once light here, and life, too. The towering land walls he stared at, waiting, were once alight with torches of the guards, who worked even at night, admitting tradesmen, travelers, pilgrims. All who knew of the Queen of Cities, the Gem of Christendom, the Apple of the World, would desire it. And so they took it.

Almost a thousand years ago, when Constantine the Great brought the Empire which bestrode the narrow world like a colossus from the precipice of ruin, he decided it should have a capital worthy of its true greatness. Rome was a city washed in innocent blood and offered to the hungers of wicked men and dark gods: it was a once-great castle built on a swamp of filth and despair. The Empire deserved a new heart, built on the power of imperial greatness and the majesty of the God of the Cross, who had brought Constantine victory and dignity to even the lowest slave. In this place between Europe and Asia, he paid dearly to every artist and holy man to fill his City with light, glory, and beauty. He made an abode of light, driving back the darkness. And so it was a safe place for him, to hide from the sins of his past. For a time.

Staring at the dumb gates hanging silently in their place, the watcher wondered what they were even there for any longer. To keep people out? To keep something in? To fool those who wanted it back that these walls, erected by the titans of old, could care to protect the desperate men who now hid inside them?

Dust swirled in the derelict road below. The howl of the wind was answered this grave-quiet night by a rending iron groan. One of the gates touched the ground, its hinges too brittle to try any longer. It staggered for a moment, then collapsed into the road.

Far away in the City, under the same dying moon, a towering bronze statue of a man long dead stood atop his massive column. Though long dead, he dreamt that this grand testimony to his greatness would lord over the low men that had to pass beneath his shadow for all time. Though long dead, he would always be wreathed in the glory of this world. Still he sat on his cold horse, arms raised in triumph, eyes staring over his empire, reigning over a dead world.

When the gate collapsed from its own weight, there were none here alive that noticed. The air grew still.

From the outer darkness entered a distant cry, muffled in the silence of the night. Men for whom this City, this Desolation, was their Dream. With God on their side, they could have it once more!

Better to have let God keep it.

Constantinople, 8th of May, 1202

All the nobles and great men of distant courts bowed down once the sitar began playing. High and powerful all these men were, to be sure, but they assembled at the whim of the Emperor, God's Viceroy on Earth, the Man Who Was Equal of the Apostles. Few dared look up to see the older man walk by them to his throne in the East, the blazing sun at his back, much less see the diamonds and precious things sway with his steps. Basil felt the others cringe when the golden lions of the throne roared their acclamation.

As the flute began to sing, the sitar fell silent, allowing the men to rise once more. Standing at the foot of the Imperial Throne, a gigantic Ethiopian banged his silver stave on the marble floor, bellowing, "ALL HAIL THE MOST AUGUST EMPEROR ALEXIUS THE THIRD, PRINCE OF THE NEW JERUSALEM, EMPEROR OF ALL THE ROMANS, DEFENDER OF THE ONE TRUE FAITH!"

"HAIL!" they acclaimed.

The old man, clad in purple and gold, looked pleased, muttering to his herald, "Very good, very good, my good Menelik." He smacked his lips languidly, his voice barely rising. "Welcome my good men. May the Lord of Hosts bless and keep you," He finished His greeting, uninterested. "So, what do We have for today?" He muttered under His breath.

A shrew of a man appeared as if from nowhere to kneel at the Emperor's left heel. "Your Majesty, the Duke Philip of Swabia, husband of Your niece, has sent a delegation to pay homage to the Gloried Throne," he whispered.

"Ah. Swabia. That's in the Germanies, isn't it?" asked the Emperor, feigning interest.

"Yes, Your Majesty."

"Very well. See them in. Be quick about it."

The advisor slinked down the purple-tiled dais to the leopard-clad Ethiopian, whispering the Emperor's wishes.

BANG.

"THE EMISSARIES OF THE COURT OF SWABIA WILL ADVANCE AND PAY HOMAGE TO THE GLORIED THRONE!" bellowed the Ethiopian.

A delegation of four men in brown brocade trimmed with fine pelt walked to either side of the crimson carpet meant only for the Emperor's feet. The men were proud and clean-shaven, and each seemed to bear the authority of those who had faced great odds. These qualities were ill-suited to the threats before them.

The four bowed in unison, the leading eldest beginning to speak. He wore long, silver hair, aged by war and tragedy beyond his years. "Your Majesty, Emperor Alexius, of the - "

"THE DELEGATION WILL PROSTRATE THEMSELVES BEFORE THE GLORIED THRONE OF THE MOST BENEFICENT EMPEROR OF ALL THE CHRISTIANS, ALEXIUS THE THIRD!" interrupted Menelik.

Taken aback, the leader asked, "I understand that those tied by marriage to this Imperial Court simply bow before the Throne."

"YOU GERMANS WILL LIE ON YOUR BELLIES BEFORE THE EMPEROR, BEGGING HIS GENEROUS ACKNOWLEDGEMENT!" shouted Menelik. The black man lowered his bellow to a snarl, finishing, "Only when He so generously grants it may you, and you alone, kneel and pay homage!"

Basil stood with his companions, Nicetas and Dukas, watching intently from outside the spectacle. Showmanship and the gentler forms of intimidation were common tools of the Roman court. Public humiliation of a kinsman's embassy was not.

"I will do no such thing," bristled the ambassador. "I, Henry of Swabia, brother by marriage to this Court, will do no such thing! My brother, Duke Philip, sent me to bring words of greetings from him and glad tidings from his wife, not to worship a man!"

The Emperor Alexius lazily interfered, saying, "Ah, but only He Who Dwelleth in Heaven deserves such adoration, dear Henry. I am but His Appointed and Humble Servant in this world. Being family, you may kiss the Ring as a show of familial fidelity," He said, extending His arm slowly forward. "Your attendants will lie down before the Throne."

An old soldier himself, Count Basil knew what just happened. The self-indulgent Emperor Alexius III, who only came to power by blinding and imprisoning His own brother, was making a show of strength to His Court at Duke Philip's expense. Weak as the empire was, this seemed a terrible decision.

Henry, if he had any doubt before, saw the same thing. Nodding to his men, these proven men lowered themselves onto the cold, glittering marble under their feet. Henry advanced to kiss the Emperor's Hand, only to be stopped short by the clenched fist of the Ethiopian.

There was a ring on it. The golden seal of the Caesars.

Reluctantly, he kissed it.

"Welcome, brother Henry of Swabia," drolled the Emperor, much pleased. "What good news do you bring Us?"

Scarcely able to hold back his disgust, Henry held up two scroll tubes. "Your fair niece bids You good words, Your Majesty. She is pleased with the court and considers her new home a bounteous country."

The advisor scurried down to snatch her sealed letter.

"And the Duke Philip, Your Brother, Your Majesty, bids You God's blessing. He also sends word of a more urgent matter. He has discovered that some of the Slavs are enflamed with lust for loot and have eyes on Your European domains. If you will have it, the Duke Philip offers to raid their flanks if You will march against them."

The advisor snatched the second tube greedily and skulked away.

"It is most generous of Philip to offer his enthusiasm, but We have no such need for his scant efforts. The Court is well aware of the wanderings of the barbarians. Indeed, We find Our Country once again beset by the dumb brutes of the races of men. To end this, We will make such a grisly example that they will all know their proper place again."

Henry responded soberly, "Your Majesty, Your Brother the Duke Philip sincerely wishes to aid Your Empire in this. Even now the men of Bulgaria prepare to –"

"That is fine and well, Henry," dismissed the Emperor. "I am glad you came this day, for you may witness and so tell Philip how the wild hordes were brought low by Our Will. Within the year, We will send forth a mighty host to drive the pagan Turks from Anatolia. Perhaps then, We may give Christian charity to your country men you left without succor in the

Holy Land." Shifting his gaze from the emissaries to the further assembly, Emperor Alexius waited.

BANG.

"COME FORTH, COUNT BASIL ARGYRUS, AND BE RECOGNIZED BY THE MOST AUGUST CAESAR, ALEXIUS, EMPEROR OF ALL THE ROMANS!" pounded Menelik.

Basil had not expected this.

Chamber of War, Blachernae Palace, later that day

It doesn't really matter how slowly you drag your palm across your face: the damn thing you didn't want to deal with will still be there when you're done.

"Unless you want to be the scandal of the whole empire, you might as well accept it, Basil," tittered Andronicus Palaeologus, the Emperor's Chief of the Armies.

Basil knew the Chief's qualifications for the role: he had never once campaigned with an army, knew not one soldier, had never been in a fight, and had never left the comfort and security of the city walls wrought by Theodosius' genius centuries ago. And he was Emperor Alexius' most ardent sycophant.

Count Basil Argyrus was a provincial lord and generally stayed away from the cesspool of politics in the capital, and it was precisely because it was full of useless people who somehow convinced other useless people to join them in a rank conspiracy against everyone else. Even if the petty nobles and ministers of the court occupied sprawling palaces with exquisite gardens, like this one, the only reason they could build it was because they robbed someone else of something

11

of value to make it. There were some worthy men who strode these halls, but they were hated or assassinated by the rest. The table on which Basil's hand rested was topped with lacquered wood brought from beyond India: the price of this table alone could feed ten families for six months, or pay a soldier's wages for a year. The setting sun filled the polished chamber replete with maps of Egypt and Spain, places the Empire had not ruled for centuries, with a warm haze.

It may not remove the problem, but face-palming does make you feel like you've done something about it.

"I have not been on a campaign in some time, and what precisely is the Emperor's great plan for driving the Turkish hordes out of the half of the empire they've had for the past hundred years?" protested Basil, finally dropping his chagrin.

The Chief continued flippantly, "Count Basil, really, this is a glorious opportunity for yourself and the good of the Empire. We all know you are skilled in the ways of war, you have scored victories against the Turks before, and now is a perfect time to march against them again."

"You mean to say that taking the war against an entrenched enemy who has almost driven us entirely out of Asia is a good idea? With what army will I march?"

"Ah, yes, Basil, 2,000 mercenary infantry, 150 Cuman cavalry freshly hired from Dacia, and six transport ships, provided by Venice," blithely responded the Chief.

Incredulous, Basil asked, "Do we have no Romans fighting for their country in this war?"

Andronicus batted his eyes almost as if having a fit. "Oh, dear Heaven, no, Count Basil. War is not something for the civilized. We have the brutish nations we can command to fight one another. It is the opinion of the Emperor, taking my humble advice, that one drop of Roman blood is worth more than a whole city of barbarians left to wallow in their filthy ignorance. No, no, there are no provisions for a citizen force to go with you."

"What of provisions and baggage train?"

"Of what, Count Basil?"

"Horses and wagons to carry our food and supplies."

13

"Oh, you will have to see to that."

"ARE YOU SERIOUS?"

Non-plussed by Basil's anger, the Chief claimed, "I am afraid I am. There should be plenty of supplies you can buy or seize en route, so being limited in your maneuver by a baggage train would only hinder a clever commander such as yourself. And think of all the riches you'll be able to plunder from the reconquered lands!" he dazzled the frustrated warrior, hands waxing like sparkling coins falling from the sky.

Basil knew that covering his face with his hands would not make the problem go away. What else could he do?

The Chief pepped up, "OH! We will be late for the Emperor's Party! He's hosting the saucy actors and the charioteers for the Green team tonight! It should be smashing, as He spared no expense!"

It still didn't help, but he wished it would.

"Coming, Basil?" chimed the Chief of the Armies.

The Court of Love, twilight

Basil cared not for yet another party at the Imperial Court. While those who knew only the safe confines of this Gilded City lived for and adored them, he knew too much of the dangerous world beyond the walls.

To be sure, he was a noble of this court, landed, moneyed, honored, and pedigreed. His family could claim the Emperor Basil the Second, the Bulgar-Slayer, on whose glory and power the Empire had coasted for over a century. His forefathers had ridden with the Emperor John Tzimisces, and it had been his line that told the Emperor of the spectacle of Jerusalem, the Holy City, laid just on the horizon from where their army stood, deep within the wounded heart of the Muslim Caliphate. Tzimisces, a man who took power and glory by his own hand, humbled himself by proclaiming that he was unworthy to behold the Holy City if he could not hold it against the Saracen army marching from Egypt.

Alas, Basil could claim no such heights of grandeur for himself. His family estate lay in Anatolia, the Land of the Rising Sun, in the province of

Bithynia, between the Phrygian mountains and the Black Sea. His home was under constant threat from the Turkish hordes, and even though he never had the men to meet them in numbers, he kept his lands safe in many dire campaigns. On none of these had he received more than kind words of support from whatever man sat on the Most August Throne, but he had men of stout heart that pledged their lives and fortunes to the salvation of his home and the souls of pure Christians that relied on him. It was a lonely war he fought, but one he had preserved.

Several times, he had been asked, and so kindly compelled, to ride to the defense of the Empire in Europe. He spilt the blood of Bulgars, Serbs, and countless pagan riders from the northern wastes. Against these he had not always triumphed, nor had his men's sacrifices always been honored by the Crown for whom they had spent their lives.

But with her near, he could forget this for a time. His mind began to clear of this history of strife and future of turmoil, as he ascended each step of the vine-laced path under the starry sky. The chambers of

Irene, his love. She was a flower of a woman, a lonely beauty from a foreign land.

Irene had come to the Queen of Cities from the courts of Provence, to be the bride of an imperial cousin. He had been a noble soul, which he gave only a fortnight after their wedding on the fields beyond these very walls.

A horde of Cumans had swept down from the hoary northern mountains, ravaging all in their path on horseback. While courtiers and pretenders plotted to take the Throne and hid behind the walls, the noble cousin rode forth to save the innocents outside the walls. He had studied the art of war as part of his education, but had never been a warrior. Rather than risk his Emperor's Throne or life, he led the mercenaries that would soon abandon him to the mercies of the cruel.

The wild men broke his front line, triggering a panic and flight in his troops, who found their lives more worthy than the Emperor's gold. He and his companions were trapped and fought to their ends, bravely earning their Creator's reward.

Basil, hurrying back to the City from his estates, crossed the waters with his men too late that night to save the defenders of the City, but did scatter the looting barbarians to the winds. Count Basil ordered to most heinous torture every Cuman he captured until they gave up the mutilated body of Irene's husband. His men solemnly bore the body into the Golden Gate, met by the mourners who stayed safe within because of his shed blood.

The Emperor paid his kin honors, and also to the man who brought his body home. Basil paid a visit to the bride while she yet mourned, pledging himself to provide for the dead man's house as his penance for arriving too late. They wept together, and a fresh love bloomed from their tears.

But that was a long time ago, and time had eased their loss. Just before the invasion, Basil had lost his wife, dead with their child within. He contemplated joining them on the other side when word reached him of the City's need; the purity of carnage eased his troubled mind. Basil and Irene were older now, and though never married, they pledged their love to one another. The Emperor's tribute to Basil had been to never send her away or to marry her to another.

Her arms enraptured him from the candle-shadowed room, her parlor caressed by the night breeze. The sweet flowers of her perfume filled him, the breath from her body lifting him to that height only men who have truly loved can dare know.

"I've waited for you, my love," she whispered softly. Brushing her locks aside, he drank in her twinkling eyes. "I heard the Emperor was having a gay party, so I knew to wait for you here," she jested. Her full lips formed a smile, the red lipstick on those tender petals glistening in the dark.

"You know me too well, my heart," he smiled back.

Letting his arms clasp at her back as she draped his neck, their lips met, parting enough for only the Holy Ghost to see. Her delicate gown pressed against the rough cloth of his hunter's vestment. It was easy for them to get lost in the swirl of passion and scented oils in the air.

He prayed that was all of today's news she heard.

Placing her slight hand in his, she led him to the window, open to the glowing City sky, before setting them upon the lover's couch. Her painted fingers played with the knot of his cloak. "Have you no manners, Basil?" she smiled. "I don't want the dirt of the streets on our couch!"

"Of course. You wouldn't want me to ruin this expensive couch, you usurer."

Her mouth opened, curled in feigned scandal. His lips brought them back to their proper place.

The cloak found its place on the marble beneath them.

They curled in embrace, as the musicians hidden in the back of the room lifted the delicate tones of the water piano into the air.

"I hear that Bithynia is beautiful this time of year. Do you know anyone who might let me see it?" she asked coyly. She had never once been to his home.

"Oh, it's a nasty place right now. My peasants are in revolt again, crying about their taxes. Apparently, they think I'll ask for their blood when I get their last bit of cabbage." He had often proffered flimsy excuses to keep her from seeing his home.

There was something too dangerous out there, beyond these walls, for him to ever want to take her there. In these walls, he told himself, she would stay safe, and his.

"Well, it is true that their lord is foul, and smells of unwashed bear pelt."

"My beard was washed just yesterday, thank you," he reposted, his fingers jabbing her precisely to elicit giggles and squirms.

And so they reclined in their bliss. She had not heard of the Emperor's Grand Campaign, so it seemed. If he could keep it from her until the deed was done, all the better: she always worried when he campaigned.

She had already lost so much beyond those walls.

Magnaura Palace, Constantinople, after sunset

Nicetas Choniates enjoyed a good party! To be sure, Alexius III knew how to throw a lavish affair, even if he was already bankrupting the Empire. After overthrowing his younger brother Isaac, who had ransomed him from a Muslim prison and given him important positions at the Court, Alexius thought he could buy real loyalty by throwing money at anyone who seemed to be important. Empires and armies live and die by the fullness of their coffers, and the Roman Empire was showing signs of its excess. Nicetas should know of these things: he served as the Chancellor of the Treasury when Isaac realized he was spending and taxing the Empire into ruin.

After betraying his own brother, Alexius needed an owned man to rob his people blind for him, and Nicetas gracefully tendered his resignation. Oh, a little graft and making sure certain friends found gold coins waiting for them for favors paid is fine, but not on this scale. As the coachman pulled to a stop outside of the palace, Choniates the philosopher prepared for a night of revelry and witty duels. There would be more temptations in this one gathering than most people face in a lifetime. It is said that virtue untested is not really virtue at all. Nicetas had settled for being found wanting. And why shouldn't he enjoy it? Someone else would pay the price.

He strolled past the peacocks, glimmering in the light of the olive lamps. He and a party of senators were led to the garden facing the sea, and none of the senators objected to his scandalous touches on their wives. One of the joys of philosophy, Nicetas mused, was that it could be used to confuse the minds of men: done properly, a philosopher could convince a faithful woman that cheating was the highest form of loving fidelity, a priest that trembling blasphemy was the only way to curry God's favor, and that acceptance of the most shameful acts was the hallmark of morality. And to think, his father had sent Nicetas and his brother to learn a righteous education in this City. At least it had worked on his brother.

Nicetas did not always use his powers for evil, but some company preferred it above others.

The African obelisk set in the midst of the garden dwarfed all in attendance, as well as the bronze animals that circled it in the fountains. "Ah, a good crowd tonight," Nicetas thought. Already, a pair of lovers was writhing in drunkenness in the reflecting pool, their soaked white garments slipping away from what little decency they had.

Nicetas was startled by the sudden appearance of the dark-browed grin of his friend, Alexius Dukas. Nicknamed "Mourtzouphlos", which means both "bushy-browed" and "sullen" in the original, Dukas possessed both characters of the word. He was shrewd enough to climb to the heights of power in the Empire, all the while in a fury about the decadence and lack of any sensibility in its ruling class. His family was quite guilty in this public shame, since they produced several emperors, not all of which were worthy of the title.

Dukas had personally waged two expeditions against rebels in the Empire, for both Isaac and Alexius, and rode with Count Basil to fend off the Turks on occasion. Nicetas came to trust the man when he put down a conspiracy at Court against Choniates, while he was busy stabilizing imperial affairs in Philippopolis after a disastrous war with the Germans.

Dukas' problem, as the Court came to see it, was that he couldn't really be trusted: he could so rarely be bought, and he kept so few mistresses. He wasn't like the rest of the Court at all.

"Hail Caesar!" Dukas gave with a mock salute, enjoying the sarcasm.

"Hail Caesar," said Nicetas, waving his hands about in mock awe of the invisible Emperor. "Has the Emperor arrived yet?"

"I haven't seen anyone being pulled on a sled by mechanical bulls tonight, so no. Is Basil coming?" Dukas inquired.

"You know he can't stand these things. I'm surprised you come, considering all the iniquity and moral turpitude to which you bear witness, and so tacitly approve of, at these parties," the philosopher teased his stoic friend.

"You want to touch me? Is that why you keep coming to these parties, hoping I will give in and you will have your chance?" roared Dukas, his rough hand grasping Nicetas by his long goatee.

Nicetas did not approve of violence, at least when it involved him, he wasn't winning, and featured a bigger man. Wincing his back up, he hated it when Dukas escalated the only way he knew how.

"Take it back," Dukas offered politely.

"LAY DOWN WITH DOGS AND WAKE UP WITH FLEAS!" defied Nicetas.

Considering this for a moment, Dukas realized he was a little flea-bitten and released his prisoner. Now safe in the knowledge his beard wasn't about to be ripped from him, Choniates joined his friend in a laugh.

The two continued on their way to the obelisk, which offered the best heights from which one can look down on their fellow man, especially gratifying if your fellow man is a divinely-ordained, irritating, and grasping ignoramus. The two men ascended to the viewing platform that rose some twenty feet from the ground, barely a fifth of the way up the colossus, alone and away from the chattering sycophants below.

After the announcement of Basil's appointment at Court earlier today, all three men had been in shock. Only a few days earlier, Dukas had held his nose and began working with the Chief of the Armies on imperial strategies for a potential campaign to be waged at some time in the future. Basil had stayed at a polite distance from the Emperor and his

Court, offering his respect when needed, defending his borders when the Turk reared his accursed head, and avoiding the lot of these vipers when he could. Nicetas, while loyally shirking opportunities to serve his Empire at every turn, used his glib-tongue and prying ears to help his companions and himself where he could. To all three, the declaration of war came as a complete surprise.

"Were your strategies so pathetic that the Chief of the Armies decided he couldn't trust your entire generation with the task, and found the last general that had not gotten all his men killed to do the job?" Nicetas asked.

Dukas shook his black beard. "We had been discussing an expedition to reclaim Cyprus from the rebel emperors, and I've been speaking with the ship makers' guild the past few days. Is there any in your higher circles who would have suggested such a thing: a land war with the Turk when the army is in such disrepair?"

Choniates quaffed his wine, "I'm afraid a plot is afoot. Consider that the Emperor declared in public, very late in the year to adequately prepare for campaign season, a general that he hadn't consulted and barely knows to lead a pittance of men laughably termed an army, with no supplies, against our most implacable and capable foe. This reeks of a set-up to me."

Nicetas spied a crowd gathering around the lovers in the fountain, more passing through the palm trees surrounding the waters to behold the licentious enjoyment. On the night air, he could smell the burning intoxicants of the Far East and see the smoke wafting from the cover of the palms. He knew they did not hide from fear of discovery or condemnation: it just made the experience more fun, pretending that anyone cared about their illicit indulgence.

Dukas mulled it over. "This could be a way of making sure that Basil either dies without the inconvenience of assassination, or stays away from the City for a long time. To what end, do you think? He has no great position in the court, and few here have the stomach to hold and defend a province as dangerous as his."

"Hmm, he does have one valuable thing in this City," the courtier let the words out to hang in the air.

His companion thought for a moment. "Irene," stated Dukas. "Nicetas, I don't like this. Basil is a good man, and he is a pillar of this Empire. Men like him, who ask so little and give so much, are what this Empire needs, like his uncle of yore, the Bulgar-Slayer!" His mind working with this new possibility, Dukas concluded, "We must help him. Can you discover the villain possibly behind this? You know their ways far better than I. I will begin assembling a force to campaign with Basil. What he is being given is enough to make the Turk mad, but not enough to stop the enemy from laying waste to all he reaches."

"Of course, Dukas. Had it not been for him, Athens would be short a bishop, and I would be without my dear brother. I do not need reminding of the time Basil rescued him from the Turk. Not a moment to waste for us, comrade," said Nicetas, hoisting his empty chalice in salutation. "If I'm to sail this wine-dark sea of sin and betrayal, I better get at it," he finished, sliding off his perch on high.

At that moment, a trumpeting of brass horns blew in the garden, signaling the arrival of the Emperor Alexius III. Heralds cried his name, and the peacocks sang. Two great bronze beasts spewing flames trod down the marble path, a jeweled throne astride their shoulders. On it sat the Emperor, loosely clad in a tunic of rubies, holding a golden chalice aloft in his left hand. He was clearly already drunk.

The partiers saluted him, some wishing his health, others his death. All were drowned out in the din his horned steeds made, so they could speak freely. So long as he felt them adore him, that was all that mattered. He begged the Empire's enemies to rob him of less, and he let the vices of every man run rampant without thought of hindrance within It, so what did it matter if he didn't really know what they thought of him? He was Caesar, and they must render unto Caesar that which Caesar wants.

God can collect his own for himself.

Venice, 15th of June, 1202

"ATTACK EGYPT?! IT'S A CRUSADE: YOU KNOW, THE THING YOU DO WHEN YOU WANT TO REGAIN THE HOLY LAND?"

"ARE YOU SAYING THAT KING RICHARD DOESN'T KNOW WHAT HE'S TALKING ABOUT? HE WAS JUST THERE! IF WE WILL EVER HOLD JERUSALEM, WE NEED EGYPT!"

The Senate amphitheater was in an uproar. The cacophony of men who were used to feeling important swung back and forth like tides across the white marble stairs. This house of debate was typically a place of deliberate plotting and quiet scheming, for the good of the Republic of Venice and the important men doing the scheming. That was not tonight.

As was understandable when people talk about holy wars, all those in attendance were a bit emotional on the issue. They were, after all, far from home, deciding when and where they may voyage only to lose their lives and fortunes, and all for the defense of Christ's City. Passion deserved a seat at that table.

31

"Gentlemen, we are all Christians here," growled the old, blind Enrico Dandolo, Doge of St. Mark's Republic of Venice. "Christ knows the ardor in your heart, but we must save the battle for the infidel," he soothed the uproarious crowd.

As the agitators settled down, he croaked, "That is more to the better. We are all agreed on the highest, noblest goal for which a man may go to war: to defend the innocent, make safe the way for the faithful pilgrim, and to recover the City of Christ's Passion. Some argue for the merits of going first to Egypt, the stronghold of the Adversary; some argue for the merits of securing the blessings of the Church of the Nativity first. Good and noble men, know that Venice will sail in the cause of Christ, no matter where the wind blows our sails! But it is not meet, my friends, for us to bicker so! Surely, the Adversary delights at our unrule!"

"HEAR, HEAR!" exclaimed the knight at his side on the stage before the assembly. The fair Count Geoffrey de Villehardouin slung his long hair aside before he continued. This meeting was critical for the eventual success of the Crusade, being the fourth such adventure, and it owed so much to him that it had made it thus far. "Knights of Christ, the Serene Doge speaks well! Let each camp select a champion in this most worthy of all causes, and let each man be inspired by the Holy Spirit, so we may know the true path our sacred quest must take! Let us recess, to choose."

The assembled nobles resumed a subdued tumult, as Geoffrey turned to the blind Doge, rubbing his blonde beard in frustration.

"Patience, Lord Geoffrey," grumbled the towering elder to his younger compatriot.

"Most wise Doge, I fear for this holy enterprise. Were it not for your timely words, any one of these powerful men may take offense and withdraw their support. I pray this does not come to pass."

"Fear not, de Villehardouin. One need only know how to command such men. Had I a care for Egypt or Canaan, the debate would be done. But we must let these men resolve their spirits into a common sword. Rest assured Venice stands with the Pope and all true Christian lords: we will sail our hundred ships for the Cross."

Descending the stairs to the pulpit, the papal emissary, Cardinal Peter of Capua, was followed by a young man whose eyes blazed with hopeful trepidation.

"Well met, Your Eminence," bowed Count de Villehardouin, followed by the Doge.

"These proceedings meet with the Blessed Father's approval," granted Cardinal Peter. "Have you given consideration to this young man's offer?" he said, indicating the well-dressed, dark-haired youth behind him.

Geoffrey dismissed the young man, "Go away, Alexius Angelus. Leave this place: we do not wish to aim our lances at our fellow Christians, no matter how misguided they are."

"Yes, we have heard his pleas, Cardinal," spoke the Doge. "Venice feels for his deposed and imprisoned father, Emperor Isaac, but the Republic is far too committed to this Crusade, even if it would help our wayward cousins in faith."

"Good, fair Dandolo. The Holy Father, while much desirous of the return of the Greeks to the

Catholic fold, does not want open warfare with the sitting Emperor," the Cardinal agreed.

The young man, who had sat quietly spying on the conversation, could hold his peace no more. "Gentlemen, I implore you! My father will support you with all the wealth and power of the Roman Empire. We will grant land to 500 knights, pay your sailors 10,000 talents of silver, and seek the forgiveness of the Father Church, if you will but right this sacrilegious injustice! He is the rightful Emperor of the East, and it took villainy most foul by his accursed brother to cast him in chains! The people hate – "

"That is ENOUGH, young Angelus!" interrupted Geoffrey. "Now be off with you before I cast you into the sea myself! We are faced with enough trouble by the infidel, we need find no new enemies," he roared, advancing with fist raised at the youth.

Young Alexius flinched, but did not cower. He silently withdrew, taking a seat with the crowd. He had only sad choices before him without these men's help: return to Constantinople and no doubt be strangled to death on his uncle Emperor Alexius III's orders, or wander from court to court in the West, living on others' grudging charity. This was his only chance to avoid those miseries, and he knew it.

As he took a seat, the two camps advanced their champions, who met with the approval of de Villehardouin. And so they met in a battle of oratory, extolling the worthiness of their cause.

The champion of the assault on Egypt spoke first. "Had King Richard III, the Lionheart, who did battle with Saladin himself, not just come back from the Holy Land? Had he not fought from Syria to Canaan and brought succor to the Christians embattled by the Saracens? Did he not gain the measure of the infidel and his unholy strength? The Lionheart knew that the Holy Land will never be safe with the enemy in possession of the unending wealth and manpower of the Nile. With our might assembled and the Blessing of the Almighty, we may take Egypt, gain this advantage for ourselves, and so break the infidel's back!"

The champion of marching on Jerusalem spoke next. "Once our forefathers marched across Europe and Asia, in blistering heat, attacked at every turn by the infidel Muslims and betrayed by the Greeks. But God Almighty kept them, and our enemies were laid low by

36

His Might! As humble warrior-pilgrims, they entered Jerusalem and rescued the faithful and the Patrimony of Christ from the torments of the heathens. And then we turned our backs on our brethren, left them to the marshalling hordes of the Muslims, and the blood of our fathers and the Will of God was undone! We cannot distract ourselves from the true cause: we must avenge our fathers and brothers, my fellow knights! Let us not waste our strength and treasure in any cause that will not save the Holy Places!"

With the two positions thus clarified, Dandolo rose and spoke, "Gentlemen, our Christian brothers have spoken well this night. Let us take their words, reflect in prayer upon them, so that God Almighty may show us the truth in our hearts! We adjourn this night, but let us return on the morrow. Then, we shall decide."

The Cardinal then rose and led the assembly of knights from across the West in prayer. With the benediction concluded, the men assembled began to leave behind their day of wearisome debate, even as one grizzled traveler quietly entered, walking against the exiting tide.

"Brother Henry of Swabia, welcome to the Serene Republic," said Geoffrey, raising his arms in greeting to his weary friend.

Henry clasped Geoffrey with hearty welcome and said, "All is not well in the East, brother. The Emperor's arrogance and stupidity know no boundaries." Henry unleashed his frustrations with Emperor Alexius III, the humiliation Henry suffered at his hands, the despicable acts he wrought on his brother Isaac, and his foolhardy adventures in Anatolia that would soon waste many lives. The picture that Henry, an astute judge of the affairs of state, had just painted showed a court in complete disarray, building up for itself an impending disaster of epic magnitude. Alexius III was setting the stage for him to lose his own throne, and he was obviously too great a fool to stop the inevitable opportunist who would pluck the Jewel of the World for himself.

The Doge, de Villehardouin, and the Cardinal listened attentively. When Henry's tirade ended, Dandolo turned to Geoffrey, quietly asking, "Is the boy still here?"

Geoffrey looked past Henry's shoulder and spied the prince-in-exile still sitting on the front row, staring at them, desperation evident in his eyes.

"Why, yes. He is."

"Good. Bring him to dinner. We have much to discuss."

Count Basil's study, 18th of June, 1202

"Nicetas, my friend, is there anything but folly in this expedition?" asked Count Basil, sharpening his blade with a wet stone.

"My dear Basil, it is a promising sign that the Emperor is even aware that the Turks exist, to be honest," replied Choniates, a half-filled tumbler in his hand, as he unfurled a map of Anatolia on the table. "But a few thousand against the Turks? That's just enough to anger them into mobilizing a horde to ravage what's left of the Empire in Asia. At best, we could seize a few border towns and a fort, assuming the sultan does not take one look at you and surrender," Nicetas finished, admitting to the possibility.

Basil did not share the mirth. "The Christians in Spania have been doing just that, though: seize and hold territory, little by little. It may just work."

"Certainly, if you live a few hundred years, you may just see if through," retorted the courtier. "The infidel in Spania does not have the hordes of Asia or the fruit of the Nile to put on the field, either."

Choniates' lack of respect was the first thing to make Basil chuckle that day, and he had already had lunch. "How true. I cannot help but wonder: why did Alexius III pick me to take the war to the East? I have rarely attended his parties, I am no favorite of his friends, and the army he has given me is more of an insult than an honor."

"It is an honor that at least one senator begrudges you mightily, I have come to discover. Oh yes, one of the Emperor's favorites, too. John Sevastos, in fact," informed Choniates.

"Senator Sevastos? Why? He's never led an army."

"And that is precisely why: he has spent his life in the pampered luxury of this City, reading about Alexander and Caesar, and wants to be one of them. All true men at least entertain the thought of doing battle, performing acts of valor, and receiving a triumph into the City. One cannot hang the laurels of victory above the mantelpiece without having first won a victory." Nicetas kept his suspicion of Sevastos' true aim of conquest to himself.

Sometimes the words of Nicetas reminded Basil of the weakness in the souls of the men in this place. Nicetas, for all his learning, knew nothing of

41

war or hardship. Men who hadn't read as much as he knew even less. They had never held a bleeding friend in their arms, as he slowly died for the glory of one tyrant or another. They had no concept of the suffering that made Alexander great, or made Caesar a god in death. They were great because they led men they held dear into the barbed maw of Hell: some returned, but every man paid his price.

This was why Basil hated this City. It was more beautiful than the dawn. In these walls were the assembled works of genius ever wrought by the hand of man; Hagia Sophia, Church of the Holy Wisdom, the Jewel of Heaven's Kingdom, was here in the New Jerusalem. All the wonders of Africa, the vices of the Orient, the endless sea of wine of the West: the people of this place thought of the outside world as a source of entertainment and amusement. These people lived in privilege not known anywhere else, and they took it for granted. This was why the Empire was failing.

The slamming open of his study door broke Basil's thoughts in their stream. An imperious Irene stalked toward him, clutching her skirt up as her hand maids scurried to keep up.

"Did you think I wouldn't find out, Basil, my love?!" she hurled her accusation like a dagger. "You think I'm such a recluse no one would tell me?"

Nicetas stared fixed at the enraged woman. Basil had hoped this wouldn't happen.

"You were just going home to assess your lands, was it? You need an army to look at your fields?!" she raged.

"My love, I didn't want you to worry –"

"WHY DIDN'T YOU TELL ME?!"

"I'm going to raid the Turks' lands south of my own. I know you don't like it when I have to defend my homestead."

"Defend your homestead? Really?! Quit lying to me! John told me it's a campaign on the Emperor's request. He expects you to retake Jerusalem, no doubt!"

Nicetas, who had been slowly obfuscating his way to the open door, stopped and arched an eyebrow in interest.

Basil steadied himself. "John. You mean, John Sevastos? Senator Sevastos told you this?"

"Why yes, he did. You could have let him, or, I don't know, let the Emperor's General of the East do it."

"I didn't have a choice!" railed Basil, sinking into a roar. "And why were you talking to Senator Sevastos?"

Irene pursed her lips, "HE is an old friend, and I do have friends of my own. We visit from time to time."

"VISIT? IS THAT WHAT THEY CALL IT NOW?" he spat back.

She flustered in astonishment. "And what is that supposed to mean?"

"I find it strange that you've been friends with that jealous letch for a long time, AND I NEVER KNEW ABOUT IT!"

"Are you accusing me of something?" she hissed coldly, narrowing her eyes to slits.

"I DON'T THINK I HAVE TO!" he bellowed.

She screamed back, "I come here to tell you I pray for God to keep you safe, and you accuse me of adultery. First you lie to me, then you call me a slut!"

Nicetas put a hand on Basil's arm to settle him. This snapped the Count out of his rage, enough to see the delicate woman in front of him trembling at their exchange.

"Irene, my dove, wait," he protested softly, putting a hand out to quell her boiling wrath.

"NO! Devil take you, Basil Argyrus! I won't hear you call me a whore again!" She punctuated this by storming out, her maids following faithfully.

Basil moved to follow, only to be held back by Choniates.

"Let her go for now. No good will come of anything more this day."

Basil looked after her fleeting shadow. His temper cooling, he felt shame come over him. "My pride got the best of me. I must tell her –"

"Her temper is as fiery as yours; it didn't take much to set you both at each other's throats," explained Nicetas. Smiling, he jested, "I see she's just as much a Greek as you are."

Casting about for an answer, the Count suggested, "I will ask the Emperor to send another. I can help supply the army, but not march with it."

His friend counseled, "Wait. I would not do that, Basil: someone is against you in the Court. Alexius III is temperamental and will not be pleased with your attempt to alter His Plans. That He did not ask you before announcing this before the Court indicates that He wanted to single you out. That He is sending so small an army shows He either wants you to fail, or He's a true fool. Now, Senator Sevastos is one of his confidants, and Sevastos wants your command and your glory. Trouble has been stirred up, and too much of this reeks of mischief to me. I have asked around, and I do not speak idle words, my brother."

Quieted by these thought, Basil heard the ring of truth in them. "Well then, Nicetas, we must plan," his eyes darting to the map. "If it is a convenient death at the hands of the Turk my enemies wish of me, we must serve them a rich disappointment." The two joined eyes, resolving to do just that.

The light treading of leather-bound feet brought their attention back to the yawning door. A dark olive-skinned man clad in silk tunic with a curled dagger at his waist stood in the breach, a sly smile on his lips.

Basil was not amused at the intrusion. "What do you want?"

The swarthy man's smile broadened, his thumbs slipping into his belt. He spoke Greek well, saying proudly, "I come with a gift for the lord of this manor. You are the Count Argyrus, yes?"

"I am."

"Good. Allah preserve you! I am a humble messenger from the man who will soon destroy your army and make slaves of your people. The sultan sends his greetings to you, his worthy opponent," the messenger punctuated with a mocking bow.

Basil and Nicetas eyed him coldly.

As the emissary raised himself up, he continued, "My lord is both generous and merciful, Count Argyrus. Your emperor is a fool, so we do not extend to him this offer, only you, for we find virtue in you."

"And what slavery does the sultan so kindly offer me?"

Taking no offense, the messenger stated, "Count Argyrus, he invites you to join him at his court, as his esteemed vassal. This empire is doomed, my

Count. Rome can no longer be ruled by emperors who send others to suffer while they indulge in all the unmanly vices. It will be ruled by a sultan, a man who will bring to it the peace of Allah and his Prophet, peace be upon him. Already the great cities of the East prosper under my lord's turban, who secures its virtues with the blood of the wicked. We invite you to kneel before a righteous lord, and in your submission, find freedom."

Nicetas fought back, "You speak of the same sultan who robs and murders innocent pilgrims who want nothing more than to pray over the bones of those who inspired hope and charity in their hearts."

The emissary dismissed this charge with a wave of his left hand. "You speak of idolaters, my good man. There is no god but Allah. Only he deserves to be worshipped. Those who reject the way of righteousness deserve to be killed. It is their blood that shows the faithful the one and true path to salvation."

Shaking his bearded head, Basil refused this, saying, "I will never renounce the truth shown me by Christ, or the love in Mary's suffering so that I might be saved. To my shame, I am no theologian, but your tradition denies all of that."

The Turk answered with cheer and vigor, "Behold, for I have good news then! Your savior did not die for you unjustly on the Cross! Allah only made it appear so, to deceive the Romans who tortured him. He was taken away, and a criminal died in his place," finished the emissary, quite pleased.

Nicetas fashioned a snare in his mind, and so responded, "So the innocent Jesus did not suffer for all us sinners?"

"No! Verily, he is in Paradise, with Allah," smiled the Grand Turk's ambassador.

The philosopher nodded thoughtfully. "Then if your prophet is right and neither Jesus nor his mother suffered for us in showing us the truth in his words, then Christ came to teach us nothing. Your prophet's Jesus was a liar and a charlatan, who, when the time to be tested for his faith came, performed a magic trick and fled like a coward rather than let his pain be a testament to the courage of his convictions. If your prophet's words are true, then neither the Redeemer's words nor his, as he claims to follow Christ, are true, and will lead only to a dark world of cowardice and fear. I ask you then, what has your master brought us?"

The Turk fumed at this slap in the face. Blasphemy against the Prophet was punishable by death in the Realm of Peace ruled by the sultan's sword. This impertinent Greek was lucky to be still safe in the Realm of War. "My lord is kind and generous to you, Basil Argyrus, not your friend. You may keep your religion. He asks only that you serve him."

Basil knew what that meant. "I know your sultan and his ways. Should I submit to him, I will serve him as a knight, but my faith as a traitor. I will have to let my churches rot while erecting his. While I may be exempt, I will have to wring from my peasants tribute money to give his imams, for their audacity to hold to their Christian faith. Finally, he will cause me to make war on my fellow Christians, to make the world a dominion of Islam and his accursed prophet Mohammed. Were I to submit to the will of your prophet, I would be a holy warrior of your untrue faith. If I keep to what my heart says is true, then I would be no better than Brutus or Judas."

The Turk glared. "Apparently you do not understand the situation presented to your lands, Count Argyrus. My lord the sultan offers you honors in his court, freedom to act as you will, and in a place where you will have only to fear dying valiantly on the field of battle, not being poisoned by a eunuch in your bath. My lord is generous and noble, and deals honestly with all who treat with him. Indeed, he will not even care that you said such rash things in this meeting: he cares only that you submit to him. In these lands yet left to the Christians, you are alone in standing nobly for the good of your faith and the innocent you protect; in the Realm of Peace, you will be counted amongst brethren. So your answer then, infidel?"

The Grand Turk was indeed mighty and honorable, for a barbarian. The promise of honor and riches was powerful, as sweet as low-hanging fruit. All it would cost was his freedom. What kind of man would make that choice? Basil confidently stated, "Let me remain a pawn in Heaven's kingdom, than be an all-powerful slave of Hell."

The Turk bowed, saying this at last. "Very well. You have made the wrong choice. I hope to place your head on my own spear. Good day." With that, he left.

The war had begun.

Forum of Augustus Caesar, 22nd June, 1202

Alexius Dukas walked down the ancient cobblestone avenue through the heart of the City, absent-mindedly slapping his riding gloves against his palm. As he passed by the splendid fountains and the heroic bronze statues of demigods from ages long past, he noticed not the throng of people coursing around him. He was entrenched in his thoughts: what devilry was even now befalling his friend; what could he do about it; and what would it take to save the Empire from its wretched state? He knew that only a little over a century ago, it was his family that brought the Empire to the precipice of ruin, and it was only strong men like Basil that kept it from crumbling while his ancestors slit throats for the Crown.

Dukas was ashamed by these crimes he never committed, as if the sin-debt for the betrayal of one good man long ago was his responsibility to pay. His family disgusted him, still carrying on as if they were slighted that their treacherous kin were robbed of the throne. Never mind the person who robbed them of it was one of those precious few men who wanted the helm only so he could steer the ship clear of the rocks, at least for a while: the civil wars his family caused and that lost Anatolia to the Turks were stopped only by Alexius Comnenus, who became Emperor by his own hand. It still surprised Dukas to this day that Comnenus had not been sainted for saving the Empire when it had more enemies than it did soldiers.

The Angelus family that now polluted the Throne had caused an uprising by the people in this City that overthrew the Comnenus line, with Isaac taking the throne. Years after his coronation, as a token of gratitude for being ransomed out of a Turkish prison by Isaac, his older brother Alexius let Isaac see what it was like to be a prisoner with no hope of salvation, only ever breathing in darkness until it choked the sanity from his mind and the humanity from his soul. For Isaac saving his life, Alexius took his sight. "No good will come of these bastard Angelus," Dukas thought.

He walked these streets as though the sun was already eclipsed.

He emerged from his meditations as he neared the object of his visit, the Syrian bandit, known as Diogenes Akritas. Akritas was the master of the market for violence on a massacre scale, having bought the monopoly for organizing the mercenary exchange in Constantinople from Alexius III. Since he was no longer in Syria, the once-lean scavenger had grown corpulent, jewels squeezing his thickening fingers, and the oil he rubbed in his graying beard fragrant enough to cover for his goatish scent. He reclined on a Berber couch beneath the shade of the four triumphal arches, slaves' fans chasing the heat away from his sweaty brow. He raised himself up when he recognized Dukas.

"My friend, Alexius Dukas, welcome! It is always good to see you, especially on this fine day. Please, sit," he said, indicating a cloth chair, "sit, and have some dates with me."

"Master Akritas, you look well. I trust your family is well?" returned Dukas, taking the proffered dates in his right hand, after shaking the thief's hand.

"Oh, they are always good. The boys are strong like their father, the women are obnoxious like theirs mothers, and business is good," he finished, as he spat out a date stone. "What else can I ask for?"

"That business stays good, my friend. I come today for just that reason, because I see you getting skinny, and I worry about you," joked Dukas, a liar's grin on his face.

"What are you looking for that I can help you with, my friend? Do you intend to take my home back for Christ?" asked the Syrian, performing a crossing of himself while he spoke. There was no way to tell if he did it out of mockery or sincerity.

Dukas shook his bearded face as he consumed another date. "I only want to do my part in support of a great man, Akritas. The Emperor has commanded my good friend Basil, Count of Bithynia, to take the war to the Turk, and then He made a joke of it by sending just over a dozen men in place of an army. I want good soldiers, so I can take them to fight by my friend's side."

Akritas' countenance fell, and his eyes came to rest on the stones under their feet. He shook his head. "I offer you dates, because that's all I have to offer. The Emperor's man has all of my stock marching for your friend right now."

Dukas disbelieved him. "You, Diogenes Akritas, the nastiest war profiteer in the history of slave-masters? You have nothing else to offer for good coin?"

"No," he replied curtly.

Dukas persisted, "Let us be fair here, Diogenes. I know for a fact that there are at least four times as many barbarians under arms in this City looking for work as we speak."

"They are already taken," said Akritas suspiciously, as he moved to stand up.

"By who? I will pay twice their offer in gold!"

Akritas gestured for the slaves to pack up and follow him, although he began walking away abruptly. He headed for the road towards the colossus of Justinian, astride his horse on that high column. Justinian held an orb in his hand, signifying the world he made himself master of; the emperor who restored the whole of the empire, by defiling it all equally.

Dukas arose in defiance. "What is the meaning of this, Akritas? You have always delivered before, and this time a good man's life is on the line! What are you not telling me?"

Akritas turned to face Dukas, a look of loss on his brow. "If there was anything I could give you, I would, my friend. Your coin is good, and your feast table better, but there is nothing I can do for you, or your friend. It's out of my hands. Go with God," he finished, as he turned and briskly disappeared into the crowd.

Dukas could not believe what he was hearing: a trader in human wrath could not be bought.

Nicetas Choniates was going to do some investigation, and he knew just how to arm himself for that: lots of liquor. As he walked behind the attendant to the lair of the Chief of the Armies, Andronicus Palaeologus, he checked the bottle of herbal liquor brought from the court of Hungary, as if to make sure it were a deadly enough weapon to get what he wanted. Remembering the last encounter he had with the dram, he was sure of it.

The servant opened the white linen veil leading to Andronicus' personal haunt, his den of pleasure. The floor was covered with soft pillows, which surrounded the feet of the plush couches in the room. The center of the room held a low pool of water, shallow enough to prevent most from literally drowning in their intoxication, but deep enough to add pleasure to any occasion. At the moment, only the wane minister lay on any of the couches, his usual escort of actors and actresses notable by their absence.

Andronicus stammered, "Nicetas Choniates, what a pleasant surprise. I do hope you're not looking for your witty jousting today, because I am just not up to the task."

Nicetas walked to the edge of the pool, a delectable smile spreading across his face. "Then I will be kind this time, dear Andronicus. However, as punishment for the debauchery you enjoyed without me, I will force you to devour this bottle with me."

"Oh mercy, Nicetas," protested the minister. "What have we here?"

Nicetas stalked closer, realizing this will be easier than he thought. Perhaps he will get the lion's share of the German's brew this afternoon. "A very thick and powerful brew made by the witches of Hungary. I cannot guarantee that children were not sacrificed under the full moon in the making of this, but even if they were, it's too late to help them now."

Andronicus lifted himself up, taking the bottle in hand. "Just pouring it into the sea will not bring the children back. We may as well enjoy their sacrifice," intoned the Chief enthusiastically.

Nicetas began pouring the drinks. In the Court of Alexius III, Emperor of All the Romans, there were two ways to make things happen in your favor: gold, or licentiousness. Nicetas was a man accustomed to pleasures but without an income, so licentiousness would have to do. Not that he was unemployable, just that he rather believed Alexius III would liquidate his brother's old ministers, to make sure no partisans tried to strangle him in his sleep. While Nicetas had been wrong, he also enjoyed knowing his blood would remain inside of him.

As the potent brew burned drink after drink down the nobles' gullets, Nicetas maneuvered the Chief of the Armies effortlessly around the conversation. He was here to find out who cast Basil the black die, but he wanted to keep somewhat circumspect. If these people knew you cared about something, they could make sure you suffered for it.

Remembering his purpose, through the din of their drunken laughter, Nicetas asked, "So what the hell happened with the Anatolia campaign? Who decided it was a good idea to send a forty year-old grump with some slant-eyed mongoloids to fight the Turk?!" he finished with a laugh.

"Ah, well, you see, well, oh my God..." giggled off the Chief of the Armies. After he regained a semblance of composure, he continued, "Nicetas, Basil was really the only choice for the campaign. He is the only general we have that has actually won sizeable battles with the Turk, he has a stake in the game, what with his home on the border, and he is so isolated politically, I figured he was a safe bet to send off with an army."

Nicetas' mind was taking all this in at full speed, the alcohol a thin patina over his thoughts. So the Chief of the Armies thought Basil was the man least likely to turn back on the City with his army and try to take the Crown for himself. Interesting.

"But why so few mercenaries, Andronicus? I think the Emperor has more cooks than that! That is really a pitiful showing for good ol' Rome, isn't it?"

"Well, we do not have the money for anymore, unfortunately. Really it is, but what with paying off the Hungarians, the Germans, the Bulgars, the Venetians, the Genoese, the Russians, Arab pirates, this was all we could afford. The Turks happened to be the ones demanding the least tribute, so they seemed like the best ones to fight."

Nicetas was disgusted, but not totally surprised by what he heard. "How sad is it, Andronicus, that Rome, Mighty Rome, is paying tribute to these barbarians?! BARBARIANS, Andronicus! I remember in the days before the Dukas clan betrayed Romanus IV, WE used to collect tribute. WE had it brought to us by groveling barbarians. Now we pay off the barbarians and make our own kin grovel in our Court. What are we to do, Andronicus?"

The Chief of the Armies shrugged nonchalantly.

"Is that all you have?" demanded Nicetas, real anger in his soul.

Andronicus grunted indifferently. "Come now, are you going to pour the rest of that or not?"

Dukas was even more pressed to find a real answer, anything he could do to help this foolhardy cause, and now. A day after Akritas fled his offerings, Dukas pondered the vexation facing his friend: men from Basil's estate came with word from a Turkish ambassador, proclaiming that Basil could either convert to Islam and join with the Grand Turk, or even his goats will be slaughtered on his church's altars. Basil had no time to spare, and went straight-away with the mercenaries at his disposal to meet the approaching hordes. Dukas had to come up with something.

He ascended the marble stairs to the parlor, where the old and the once-mighty congratulated themselves on their past greatness. As he entered the checkerboard black and white marble floored hall, he surveyed those around him. An assembly of some four-score men had gathered here, standing bedecked in their finery beneath the massive crystal works hanging over their heads. Musicians, slaves from the West, sat in a corner, playing their instruments to soothe their masters' ears. He found them all wonting.

Here were the scions of great houses, families with vast estates, or those with money left over from vast estates long lost to the Turk, but did not care to try to take their homes back. "That would require a measure of spine," Dukas sneered to himself. That would take getting their lily-soft hands dirty. At this particular gathering, he spied Senator John Sevastos across the room. The tall, aged man still had a full head of sandy-blonde hair atop his clean-shaven face. He was dignified in the way someone who has no idea of how his breakfast gets made in the morning is dignified. He was of one of these disinherited families, his family having lost their lands in the East over a century ago. They had been living in the capital on money somebody else had earned ever since. It did not seem to bother him at all.

Dukas took one of the crystal chalices heady with sweet red wine from the dutiful butler and walked farther in. He quaffed the libation and began to mingle. It amazed him: none of the insulated fools he spoke with mentioned the impending war with the Turk. It seemed as if they took notice of it only like a peasant noticed the City criers mentioning yet another coup in the Papal palace: of little interest, and no direct relevance. As the chalices began to empty, Alexius Dukas' rage continued to scale that high peak.

His patience wore on for almost an hour, as he swam through the sea of nobility. All he had heard were petty intrigues, or complete inconsequentialities. But upon hearing one too many accolades for the Emperor's most recent party, Dukas smashed his chalice against the unyielding floor, the shattering bringing a stark reality to the room. The old, tired faces looked aghast at him. The impetuous man climbed the dining table, a leer on his drunken face. His eyes were like an accusation at each of these worthless men.

"WHAT USE ARE YOU, OLD MEN?! WHAT USE ARE YOU? You sit here, behind the walls your ancestors paid somebody else to build, and you do what? You leech off your peasants, or your relatives, or their past. How many of you have ever gone to war for this Empire? How many have shed a drop of blood for their faith? Hm?" he grunted rhetorically.

"DO NONE OF YOU HEAR ME?! WE ARE AT WAR! WE HAVE BEEN AT WAR WITH THIS

ENEMY FOR SIX HUNDRED YEARS! A GOOD MAN RODE OUT THIS DAY TO STOP THE ENEMY THAT WILL CLAIM ALL YOUR LIVES, AND NOT ONE OF YOU EVEN MENTIONS HIM! YOU BUNCH OF WORTHLESS –"

Dukas' drunken, but very sincere, rant was cut off, as he almost fell down from a pull on his sleeve. He fought it, clumsily, but soon yielded and was drug off to a far corner of the hall, to take refuge behind a statue of the Deified Caesar, mutely clad in enough diamonds and silver to fetch another hundred mercenaries.

As Dukas leaned against the cold stone of the wall, he felt a sharp slap bring him back to himself. His eyes focused on the wrinkled countenance before him, recognizing the man. "Manuel Lascaris: how did he get invited to this party?" Dukas thought. A second slap kept him from wondering further.

"Quiet, boy!" commanded the old man, his double-braided beard shaking with indignation. "You do your friend no good by carrying on like this." Dukas' eyes drew into focus on the old man's accusing finger, shoved in his face.

Dukas had to assess the situation, let the wine clear a little from his mind. As his blood began to cool, he spoke, "You are right, sir. It pains me, to see us at these effete parties, toasting each other's glory, while my friend marches off to fight the Adversary. The Emperor sent him with nothing, and we stand by and let him go with nothing. We are kept safe because of good men ready to do and suffer violence for us. What justice is there in that?"

The old man nodded, his crow's feet showing his years. "And you wish to march with him, as you should. Real men fight for what they believe in. Do you see any of these men fighting for anything?"

"No," Dukas replied.

"Exactly. You tried to buy some mercenaries yesterday, yes? Did you know the Emperor's orders?" asked Manuel.

Dukas shook his head, his brows closing in puzzlement.

"Between you and me, the Emperor forbade any mercenaries to be sold to aid Count Basil on this expedition. He is a good man, you and I both know," whispered the old man. "I say to you this, Alexius

Dukas, the Emperor has many bought and paid for men in His Empire, and I know you are not one of them. Watch yourself. As for your friend, I know of a boat going to the Crimea soon. In the North, there are many strong men, who could stand as giants next to you or I. I suggest you take this boat, if you want to help your friend."

Dukas nodded his head quietly. Now he had found an answer.

Nicetas realized, as he turned the letter over in his hand, that the Chief of the Armies knew nothing. Dukas had told him how many swords-for-hire could be found in this City, but none to be bought. None that could be bought, by fiat of the Emperor, it seemed. It was one thing to not send more men due to lack of money; it was another to prevent them from being sent. There had to be more, and Nicetas suspected there was an ass involved.

"Senator John, how are you?!" greeted Choniates, with a great, toothy grin and hearty hand-shake. The two gathered in the Magnaura Palace, in one of the verandas overlooking the gardens and the sea beyond.

"Lord Choniates, it is good to see you well. What brings you by this day?" inquired the senator, half-rising from his reclining couch. He offered one limp hand to shake; the one with the true grip was busied holding the wine.

"Hm, what lie to pick for the occasion?" Nicetas mused to himself. "Will you accept beautiful vistas, good conversation, and a dash of something extra to elevate ourselves?" the philosopher asked, producing a wooden box inlaid with mother-of-pearl. He laid it on the table between them, daring John to look further.

The high-boned senator raised an eyebrow in interest. His long fingers reached for the box, opening it slyly. A low smile came upon his face at the sight in his hands. "Why Nicetas, where ever did you get it?"

"I know a lot of people who do not get to spend much time around senators."

The two clandestinely prepared the hashish, the conversation joining in hushed excitement. Hashish was a tool of the Old Man of the Mountain, master of the Assassins that plagued the Near East. It was said to exalt the imbiber to Paradise, where all the pleasures of this world became infused with those of the next, and the fall back to Earth could break the weak in spirit.

Whatever their faults then, at least Nicetas and John had survived the fall enough times to earn places amongst that kind of strong. The opiates swimming through their heads, Nicetas whittled away at John's existence, challenging him with paradox and ruse time and again. John wondered if he was on the verge of enlightenment; Nicetas had seen buffoons think they had made it there before as well.

In times like these, Nicetas liked to trot out the Buddhist mantra he had learned from the mystic that practiced that strange religion. Those he told of it were always so amazed, that by releasing the chains that bind your spirit to everything around you, you could be truly free. He had seen at least one marriage break because of this bit of sleight of hand; he had seen men robbed of their purse willingly for it. Nicetas always laughed at the thought: what kind of enlightenment brings you freedom in a world that now means nothing to you?

As Nicetas kept John's mind spinning and spinning, he pondered how to fish out the information he was sure would damn the senator in the scheme. Imagine his surprise when the middle-aged man started spewing it out on his own.

He spoke airily, the drugs preventing any speed or cohesion in his words. "You know, Nicetas, Irene is surely a star in the Canopy of Heaven. I remember it all like it was yesterday. Fifteen years ago, I set sail for France to settle the marriage that would tie the House of Angelus to the West. I went, I met her father, we shook hands on the agreement, and then I saw her for the first time. My God, she was beautiful! I swear even you have never seen such a marvel, Nicetas. Those pouty lips, that slim waist, those apple-blossoms on her bosom. Why, I lamented that I was going to pick up someone else's bride! Ah, those eyes, round as pearls..." John trailed off.

Nicetas was glad that John was staring at his unseen star, because the look of disdain on his face would surely betray his intent. A man he trusted as a true friend was being sent to possible death or worse, because of this vapid waif? Still, he pressed on. "Have you ever had a taste of that morsel, dear John?"

John licked his lips at the thought. "No, I cannot say that I have. Oh, how I've wanted to! But tell me for true, what man could resist even the thought? She is just as sweet to behold this day as ever beauty graced a woman."

Nicetas, a hard edge forming in his voice, asked, "You must be glad then, since her man has gone from here to fight the hordes of Asia with a few meager barbarians at his side? I suspect she will need a trusted shoulder to cry on then, won't she?"

John, oblivious to the menace growing out of his sight, smiled. "It's good to be the king. It's also good to be amongst his friends."

Nicetas, hearing what he long suspected, grasped for any mean instrument. "Why, you –"

He was cut off by the approach of a storm of servants, feverishly brushing the floor clean before the steps of the Emperor.

Nicetas and John sat straight up, their hazed vision being set ablaze by the shimmering sight of the

Emperor approaching them from the South, and His purple and red silks moving gently with the breeze.

Nicetas arose to pay homage. John reclined once more on his couch.

"Good day, Choniates, good day," the Emperor dismissed, as he sat on the couch placed that very instant beneath him by his bejeweled slaves.

John looked to the Emperor, and rendered Him the offering, "Hashish from the East, a gift from the Old Man of the Mountain himself! He knows the Emperor of All the Romans only smokes the best!" John finished, a chuckle erupting from his chest.

Alexius III looked mildly pleased as He moved to partake. Nicetas grew almost nauseated, having now seen first-hand the Emperor Himself partaking of this rapscallion's herb. The Most August of the Race of Men debasing himself like a common criminal. Or a philosopher. No wonder the Empire was doomed.

"So what are we doing today, gentlemen?" Alexius inquired, bored.

John started, "I was just telling Nicetas how fresh a blossom Irene –"

Nicetas cut him off. He stared straight at the Emperor, drug-addled head hanging low, his gaze intense. "Did you send Basil to his death on purpose?"

Alexius heard him, puffed on the dragon's smoke, then answered in His own time. "Oh, that. Would it surprise you if I did?"

Nicetas fought to keep himself from jumping at the man who witlessly was about to be responsible for thousands of deaths. He still had plenty of guards around the veranda to protect him. "Emperor, did you send Count Basil to die in the East because of this fucking tramp wanting his woman?"

Alexius exhaled smoke in a puff of amusement. John did not share it.

"Well, John, that will undoubtedly be a side-benefit, but no. I know you Choniates, you will needle the truth out of me some way or another, so I might as well tell you. Count Basil is the only member of this whole blasted aristocracy that stands a chance at my throne." Seeing the incredulity on Choniates' face, the Emperor continued, "Oh, yes, my friend. You know as well as I do, many see me as weak, and Basil is the strongest where I am seen to be the weakest. He does not spend his whole day intoxicating himself to excess, like we do, so people like that sullen Dukas boy would try to raise him up on a shield. By sacrificing one man's life, I can save a hundred thousand from death in civil war. One man is not worth all those innocent lives."

He stopped to consider the pipe in his hand. "You are right, John, this is excellent. Almost as good as my personal stock. Anyway, yes, I did send him to get far away from this Court, with too few men to do anything about it. And because he's loyal, he will do it, faithfully."

The Emperor reclined on his couch, watching Nicetas struggle with what to do. "Now the real question is: what are you going to do with that information?"

The Emperor, as detestable a man as he was, shimmered with multi-colored radiance in Nicetas' drug-addled sight. His shrinking and expanding vision beheld the dazzling Emperor wreathed in flame like a judging angel of the Lord, an awe filling Nicetas' cynical heart. "Damn," thought Nicetas, "the drugs have foiled me!" Nicetas had not foreseen this ambush;

least of all, he had never expected the Emperor to tell him the truth. Now he knew not what to do.

He did know, however, there were right and wrong answers to the Emperor's question.

"Let me help you," continued the Emperor. "My dear friend John here is sick. He is wasting away on the inside. Pining is not something a Sovereign has to do, but, alas, John is not the Anointed of God. He is dear to Me. The Imperial Academy is in need of a talented master, someone who understands learning, truth, and beauty. Someone who can lead its students and their professors to become witnesses to the wonders of man's genius and God's Creation. You are such a man, well-versed in all the noble arts and sciences. And ambitious. So I ask you, as a physician, help this dying man acquire the medicine he needs, Nicetas. I know your help will not come cheap, but it will be worth it."

"Or?" asked the philosopher.

The Emperor stared at him, cold, uncaring. Brutal.

Right or wrong.

Dukas checked the last of his belongings, and ordered his porter to take them on the ship. The sun was heavy in the early morning sky, but the weather should hold, said the withered old sea men. He had never traveled to the Crimea before; he had never been on the foreigner's home turf. He realized that all the battles he had experienced with the enemy had been on his native soil.

He turned to face Nicetas, who had come along to see him off on his journey. Nicetas comforted his friend, "Fear not for the sea voyage, fair Dukas. The Greeks of old called these waters the 'Friendly Sea', in the hopes it would not devour them as greedily as it did. You should be fine."

Dukas did not care to joust with words today. "So is there any word from your sources on the root of this evil? I have no more time to waste asking questions of the idle."

Nicetas, playing his part, replied, "Nothing of substance. I plied John with the best grease I had. It got the best of him. The pansy passed right out on me. He admitted to admiring Irene's beauty, but even we will admit to that." Choniates hoped that looked convincing.

Dukas listened, still distracted. "Very well. Take care, Nicetas. Watch our backs."

Nicetas embraced his younger friend, then watched him slip over the horizon.

Nicetas hid the letter. He could not resolve to burn it or deliver it, so he hid it. Basil had left with him a letter for Irene just before he departed for death or victory. He asked that Nicetas, his friend, deliver it in two weeks' time. That was three weeks ago.

Irene's slave-girl showed the philosopher to the study, where her mistress lay in the waning sunlight, reading poetry. She had never written any of her own. Not because she had nothing to say, but in reading the works of others, she found that the secret chorus in her heart was already writ large in the world. It was probably better that way: if the songs were hers to write, she might keep them all to herself.

She closed the book and rose to meet Nicetas. "Welcome, good Choniates. What news do you have?" Her lips pursed, caught between a smile and a grimace.

Even in such a state, the beauty of her lips was undeniable, he saw. Refusing to allow himself the pleasure of thinking of them in such a way, he focused himself to the task at hand. "Word has it that our good Count Basil and his army have traversed the mountains of Phrygia and shocked the Turk with their advance! With his genius on the field, perhaps the war can be over and done with soon," he lied.

She bowed her head pensively. "Nicetas, you saw how we parted. I have been thinking of him so much. I just can't help it! He really is a wonderful man, when he lets me have him." She turned away from the Greek to face the setting sun. "I just don't know if he's someone I can ever hold on to."

The bribe had been very large. Nicetas mulled his situation over in his mind. Gold to refurbish his home; the headmastership of the Academy; and his own personal ship, with crew to take him wherever he wished. Money, the power to shape the minds of generations of youth, and the freedom to travel anywhere in the world he wished. Nicetas was glad for his temptations.

Irene was not privy to these bitter thoughts. "What of you, Nicetas?" she said, turning and approaching him, her dress slowly rocking back and forth. "Have you felt the pains of love and choice like this before?"

He came back to the moment, remembering he had something to do, for one price or another. "I have not been terribly lucky in love, my dear. I find women so transitory in thought and feeling, as though they have no true master, even themselves. Their intellectual curiosity is sated far too soon, whereas mine pulls me forth whether I want it to or not, like a spooked horse dragging his broken chariot. I enjoy this mind and filling it with the secrets of the universe, but sometimes I wonder if it costs more than it benefits.

"Behold, outside your window," he said, marching into the dying rays of the setting sun. "See those men there, carousing at the tavern. They are so much into the moment, they enjoy every drop of the wine in their cups! Were I to drink the same wine, I would think of its qualities, how it compares to other vintages, its significance in the grand scheme of things, and, ultimately, its smallness."

Irene placed the book of poetry back on the voluminous shelf. "Is this a clever sophistry to cover for your wanton philandering? I feel your suffering for the love of knowledge, but somehow I have not fallen into the same noetic trap as you."

She met his sharp, feigned glare with her luscious smile, standing before her full bookshelves, a rogue blonde lock hanging before her eyes.

"My God," thought Nicetas. "Basil is so lucky: to have a woman of this beauty, this charming, and a stack of books this big (that she actually reads)! I could settle for that."

Maybe I should settle for that.

Nicetas let his fake glare turn into a sly grin as he turned to her. "Irene, how long have we known each other?"

"Twelve years, if I recall correctly."

"Then you know me well. Tell me, what am I doing wrong," he continued as he stalked towards her. "Why do I drift from woman to woman, none holding my interest longer than their virtue can resist my temptations?"

Her doe eyes grew wide, as she chuckled at the challenge to explain a philosopher to himself. "Really, my Nicetas?! You ask me, a mere woman, to explain to a man why his overwhelming masculine virtues prevent him from finding and desiring just one woman?"

"Consider it a test of whether your kind is capable of spotting obvious truths invisible to mortal men," he purred, moving within arm's reach of her. How tempting it feels, to be so close, to this pearl, to be able to simply touch her. He had never been alone with her, now that he thought of it. And so close to her.

Then she was upon him! He had been lost in the scent of her perfume when she reached out and held him! His arms reacted in delay, curling around her small back. He felt the soft cloth that covered her back, the only thing between his finger tips and her bare skin. Now would be a good time to make the play.

She spoke first. "Nicetas, you old dog. You chase a scatter of women because you don't consider yourself really worthy of being had and had alone. That brain of yours is forever scouring the world for stimulation, drinking the excitement and newness out of everything it touches. That includes you."

He hadn't expected that answer. Interesting.

"But I think well of you, my old friend. You enliven this part of the world with your snooty insurrections, and it would be the poorer without it. I am most pleased that Basil has the good taste to find worthwhile friends like you and Alexius," she finished, as she dropped her hold on him and walked back to the window. "Argh, that impossible man! Perhaps you can explain your precious Count to me, Nicetas?"

Ah, a friend only he is to be? Had Basil had good taste in picking his friends?

Nicetas stood quietly. He could see she was not his for the taking. What would the Emperor do to him if Nicetas did not deliver? What else would He do if this did not go as He had wrung in agreement from Choniates? Nicetas could flee, but to what dark, inhospitable shore could he take refuge? After the light of Constantinople, what shallow harbor could suffice?

Nicetas came out of his meditation at the sound of Irene's tears. She had sat down on the embroidered couch, her back to the setting sun. He knew the tears were for the man outside the walls.

A serpent could not ask for better prey. "Okay, Nicetas," he reflected, "now or never. Is the wealth of this world worth the heart of one man? The man who had been his friend for twenty years and saved his own kin from torture and death. Or defy the man who sentenced the brother that rescued him from prison with eternal darkness?"

Well, is it?

Claudiopolis, Anatolia, 10th June, 1203

Desperately, Kamal clawed at the grass, dragging himself across the dirt with every last ounce of strength in him. His hasty escape was brought to an abrupt halt: he felt first his clothes then the searing hot flash of pain pierce the flesh of his calf. He screamed in agony, his body extending until it seemed that his free limbs would flee from his body. They were not to be so lucky.

The throbbing pain lost its pressure, and in an act of survival-driven madness, Kamal's body wanted to do something, anything, to protect itself. He had been unhorsed, now crippled, so his instincts told him to face this menace. Maybe he could dodge the next blow, then maybe the next. He knew the reality: death was here. He scrambled over, to face down this foe. He raised his arms over his body in meager defense, both limbs shaking without his permission. His killer stalked to loom over him.

The heavy spearhead tore through his face, smashing his brow to pieces, as it planted inside, extinguishing his light. Basil twisted the shaft of the spear, the crunch of the bones reaching his ears. He did not enjoy killing, not in principle: however, people often change their minds when it comes to the person out to kill them. When the fear of imminent, horrible, agonizing death comes upon him, it steels his nerves, bringing forth the primal killer deep inside the hearts of so many men.

In general, he found that people react in one of two ways when faced with death: some feel their souls twist with rage, a defiance arising within that wants to rain down every last bit of fury at Fate to save their life, even in the face of impossible odds; some freeze in place, every part of their spirit shrinking, even if full of boast and vinegar in normal times. "Perhaps," they think, "if I debase myself enough, if I give up enough of myself to this person who has no right to do what they're doing, they will, like a just god, give me mercy. Maybe I won't be important enough for them to kill."

He knew all too well what happened to those who begged when they should have fought. Standing placidly as the dagger slits one's throat does nothing to stop it; thrashing like a wild boar will at least make an end worthy of a man, maybe more. An arrow can pierce his armor, but Basil only minds the force of the impact, not the pain of the wound.

Until he comes down. When the need to react with calm and dignity to other human beings comes at last, as when seeing to the needs of the wounded and dying, he feels shame. A Christian should not kill, or at least enjoy killing, he was told. The priests would not give him or any warrior communion until the war was over. Bloodshed was not a holy act, contravening the Commandments and the example of Christ. But if Basil did not kill this young man, this Turk would kill his son, rape his daughter, and force her into slavery, sentencing her to a lifetime of crying, while the man who ruined her life fucks her every day. He wondered how many women had to carry inside of them the children of men who took them as slaves.

He thought of Irene. He always thought of Irene.

It was true, though: he had no children of his own, no flesh of his flesh. The reaper had carried his one chance away long ago. As lord of this country, though, he thought of all his people as his own flesh and blood, like fruit grown in his own garden. If killing this man was a sin, Basil was comfortable with that: the priests say he was born into it anyway.

In this life, however, his Cuman horsemen were playing with the heads of the enemy, using them as sporting balls. They rode around the plumes of smoke on the field of battle, playing a grisly game of keep-away. Evidently, they did not share his crisis of conscience. In the beginning months of the war, Basil tried to put a stop to their vicious celebrations. That had not worked out.

The cost of the battle before the walls of Claudiopolis had been high. But what choice did he have, but to perpetrate such cruel measures? He was outnumbered three to one! Had he chosen differently, how many more than the 10,000 dead here would have met wretched fortunes?

The Grand Turk, Sultan Suleymanshah, launched his war on three fronts into the Empire, intent on driving all imperial garrisons into the sea and making himself master of Asia. This act of sheer recklessness was the only thing that saved even a ghost of hope for the Empire: with the Turk's forces spread out, he could not simply crush underfoot the sad imperial army sent against him. For this folly, Basil was grateful.

When he first arrived in Asia, Basil sent his home garrison to block the pass out of the Phrygian mountains leading to the plain of Bithynia, to buy what time their lives would purchase. As bands of marauders went west towards Ephesus and east towards Trebizond, the governors of these lands were on their own: that, Basil could not help. The army he knew was marching toward his homeland was all he could deal with. A loss of either of the other territories would be a great loss, to be certain. However, if he fell here, there was nothing to stand between the sultan and the City.

The refugees that ran screaming out of the mountains he tried to help. The villages they left behind, the homes they would never return to, would be robbed and burned. Those too old or infirm to make the march had only to sit where they were and wait for death. Being physically useless for labor and unattractive to the Muslims' lust, the Turk would not bother taking them to the slave markets. At best, their suffering and piteous cries brought on by foulest tortures might provide some laughs and sick joy to their tormentors. In any event, they did not have to wait long.

As he waited for the rest of the mercenaries to arrive from Constantinople and augment his personal forces, he rode from town to town, gathering word of the enemy's movements. Word of the Turkish host breaking out of the mountains after its slow, ravaging march to the plains of Bithynia reached Basil at the edge of his domain in the east, as he fought the slaves of the Grand Turk, who had almost starved the seaside city of Sinope into surrender.

Basil caught the besieging army unawares at the break of dawn, sending terror through their ranks, causing them to flee the walls of Sinope just after the fighting started. The Count's scouts arrived the next day with word of the Turk initiating an assault on Claudiopolis, founded by Claudius Caesar himself over a thousand years ago. As Basil suspected, the Turk had only sent small bands of men to terrorize Ephesus and the same into the eastern coastal stretches of the Black Sea. He knew he needed to marshal every spear to this cause: the Grand Turk himself was on the move.

The words of the scouts, who were personal companions of Basil, weighed heavily in his mind. Should he pursue and crush the enemy, who had only freshly fled from the gates of this city? He had just visited Claudiopolis; how much food and water did it have stored away to weather a siege? What of his home and capital to the north, Heraklia? Why couldn't he recall these details? The war, the very survival of his people could hinge on the decision he was about to make. The haze of decisions and the unknown in his mind was about to drive him mad.

"Count Basil, why is your brow so troubled?"

His thoughts were interrupted, bringing his gaze from the sea below the gray stone gallery in which he stood to the mosaic floor, finally seeing the old man who broke his frustrated reverie.

"We have won a great victory just yesterday, glory be to God!" claimed Theophilus. Theophilus was a lean, wizened man; something of a tyrant, the bishop of Sinope became the champion of the city's defense when the governor fled the walls for his own safety, in fear of the duty that was rightfully his.

Basil recovered himself, pulling his thoughts out of the pit of apprehension he was exploring. "Nothing to trouble yourself with, father. Word of the enemy marching, and what to do with it. He moves on three fronts: diversions to the west and east, and what looks to be the main thrust at the City Itself across Bithynia. He drove back my guardians from the mountain passes and even now launches an attack on Claudiopolis." He finished this sentence, his voice exposing the quiet desperation in his heart.

He had been thrust into a war without the strength to fight it, and now the Turk was on his doorstep, preparing to set his house on fire.

"Why do you not meet him, smash him, and drive him before you, under the aegis of the Almighty?!" boasted the aged priest, clapping his staff against the tile floor in exclamation. "You have His Blessings, it is clear, for you saved the whole of these people, driving away the enemies of God like a scouring wind! This feat would not have come to pass without His Will."

Unabashed enthusiasm is necessary for fools, inventors, and lovers. Basil spoke his skepticism,

"Father, it is said that the Emperor wears the Crown by God's Will. He is God's Vice-Regent on Earth, the Equal of the Apostles, but I cannot see where this one has any claim to grace at all. Yet I serve him, and I am faithful. Am I not merely a lackey of the Devil's usurper, and so no better than he for enacting his will on earth?"

His bile continued rising, "I will lead men to die for his dominion, men he needlessly put in hazard. Every peasant, every tradesman, man and woman, slave and freeman that dies in this war, I feel their deaths rest on my head, because it was given to me to fight this battle for the Empire," Basil spoke plaintively. "I cannot reckon a man less worthy to be called Caesar!"

The piercing blue eyes of the bishop searched his savior's face, looking into the wrinkles and scars for the measure of the man. Pulling the gilded staff closer for support, Theophilus asked, "Do you ask, or do you tell, my Count? You show the sincerity of your faith in the torment you express, and it is right what you ponder. The wickedness of the Emperor is undeniable: only His Gold has kept Him on the Throne."

Knowing this to be true, but not wanting to be petulant at the bishop, Basil leaned toward the sea, placing his hands on the stone pillars lining the gallery. He grew animated as he pressed on, despite his intention of not appearing recalcitrant. "But is it not the inaction of men like me that keep him there?! Is he not still sitting there on the Throne, poisoning the True Faith and the Empire with His Iniquity, because men like me do not stir in our righteous wrath?!"

The bishop seized Basil by the arm, stopping him in his tracks. "Know you not that we live in the end of days, Basil Argyrus?! It has long been told that man would come to ruin before the Savior comes again! As Paul said, 'For that day shall not come, unless indeed there first come a falling away, and that man of sin be revealed,' by which he proclaims what will be the end times and the coming of the Antichrist. It is he who will sit in the church of Christ, proclaiming himself greater. Remember the words spoken by Christ himself, 'That there will come a day that there will come those that smite at the necks of the faithful, and they will praise themselves for doing work pleasing unto the Lord God!' This war is with the Mohammedans, who believe such a thing: the words of their prophet, may he rest in Hell, proclaim the beheading of those who do not submit to Islam to be pleasing to their Allah. The time is at hand!" he thundered.

Basil soaked in the power that strode forth in the bishop's voice, and it did not ease his mind. "Great," he thought to himself: "not only are my lands going to be ruined if I fail, but the end of the world is riding on me, too. Fantastic. Just fantastic."

"Father, I know you to be a man of learning and wisdom. But those sermons of the end times have been recited for centuries. Each time, the world has carried on, limping or otherwise. What real reason do you have to believe them now?"

The old priest assessed the Count, calculating behind his eyes. "Are you a man of letters? Do you have command of the tongue of the Church Fathers?"

Basil nodded his assent.

"You need not take my word for it then," said Theophilus as he turned to lead Basil away from the din of the crashing waves below. "You can read the words for yourself."

Theophilus led his companion into the catacombs beneath the church by the sea. The graves they passed by were bounded on either side by the dark waters, only a few feet of rock keeping the tendrils of the sea out. The shadows retreated and hid in the empty sockets of the dead as the priest led the Count to the object of revelation, with a single flickering torch to light their way.

Down a time-smoothed flight of steps carved into the earth, the pair arrived at the chthonic library of Theophilus. Basil stopped at the open archway leading into their destination: a pall hung in the air. What secrets did the bishop, leader of the faithful, hold down here, in this place more befitting a tomb than a library? He did not reckon himself a mason of stone, but the way in which this room was carved did not sit right in his eyes; the walls vaguely appeared to have been clawed upon all around the room. Nothing good or pure would hide in such a place.

Theophilus took no notice of his companion's hesitance, pulling from a bookshelf set into the wall a ratty, leather-bound volume, hefting it onto his rock-hewn reading ledge. The bishop licked his fingers, thumbing through the ancient pages, until he came to the passage which would enlighten the savior of his city. He quietly stood aside so that Basil might read the evidence for himself. Holding the torch aloft, he beckoned for his follower to read the words long written down.

The Count approached the tome warily, asking, "What is this that lies before me?"

"The words of the very Father of the Church, Tertullian. He who discovered to the world the truth of the Trinity of God, who spoke with the Holy Ghost within him. He was the one who taught the early fathers to wreck the devious lies of the pagans and the heretics upon the rock of Truth and to bring the Light of God to even the most determined idolater. Once an admitted heretic himself, when he was brought to the true light of the Church, he became the false idols' most formidable enemy. From Africa he came, in the days before it fell to the pagans. It was he who kept Marcian from leading the entirety of the faithful astray; he who showed the pagans of Rome and their mystery cults and bloody rites to be for false gods. So strict was his observance of the Word, he remonstrated even the pope in Rome for his laxity in his observation of the commandments. Read, and see the prophecy which will make complete your vision of the world around you."

Basil was no theologian, but he was unsure of a "Father of the Church" of whom he had never heard. Where was Nicetas when you needed him? He knew his theology, even if he rarely used it. As he scanned the Latin letters on the vellum, he read:

"And now ye know what detaineth the coming of the Antichrist, that he might be revealed at his appointed hour. For the mystery of iniquity doth already work; only he who now hinders can hinder his rise further, until even he be taken out of the way. What obstacle is there to the ascendant darkness but the baleful glory of Rome? Pray against the hopeless day, when the crown falls away! As none other who came before, this empire in damnation seals away the coming to the terrestrial sphere of the Mid-Day Devil, the Antichrist, the demon made flesh who fears not the cleansing sun. When crumbleth the universal empire, decadent and wicked, its remnants shall scatter into the ten kingdoms, none with the strength of the decaying father. Then the Antichrist shall be introduced upon its ruins, and then shall be revealed the wicked one, whom the Lord shall consume with the spirit of His mouth, and shall destroy with the brightness of His coming: even him whose coming is after the working of Satan, with all power, and signs, and lying wonders, and with all the deceivings of unrighteousness in them that perish.

Basil looked up to Theophilus, "What blasphemy is this?"

The bishop forced Basil's eyes back to the page:

"So, it is that, Babylon, as in the Revelations of our own beloved John, is verily the figure of Rome. Equally great and proud of her sway it is, the City of seven horns, filled with sin and harlots, and triumphant over the saints. Heady it is in its drunkenness with the blood of the martyrs, and filled with the power of the sacrifices rendered unto Caesar, the strength of its sword smote all that came before it. Believe you not, but there is a greater necessity for our offering prayer on behalf of the emperors, even for the complete stability of the empire, and for the might of foul Rome in all things.

For the angel told us that a mighty shock seeking to wash over and devour the whole earth - in fact, the very end of all things - is only retarded by the continued existence of that abominable empire. Yay, though the coming of the Lord be great and full of glory, His coming will be heralded by much dread and the desolation. We have no desire, then, to be overtaken by these dire events too soon; and in praying that their coming may be delayed, we are lending our aid to Rome's duration. Brethren, it is our mission to evangelize the world and bring as many souls as He allows to the Cross. Only then may there be enough faith to keep the light from sputtering out in the abyss."

Theophilus saw the look of bewilderment take root in Basil's eyes. "Know you now the full truth when Christ spoke, 'Render unto Caesar that which is Caesar's; render unto God that which is God's.' Christ did not challenge Caesar's right to rule, nor the injustice of his many bloody deeds. These were necessary, He knew, to forestall the coming incarnation of the Adversary.

"Believe it if you will, or not: what is critical is that you act with the full knowledge of the truth behind it. The Emperor, wallow in sin as he might, is the only thing standing between the world and the rise of Satan. Serve him, protect him, replace him with one more noble if you must, but fight for him! Kill in his name when you have need. While it is preferable to have a just man at the helm of the Empire, do not fail to act in the name of one who gathers to him innumerable wickedness, who cloaks himself with sin. As wicked as the Empire ever was, its injustice has kept the greatest evil at bay," lectured the priest.

Basil pushed himself away from the ledge, refusing to accept this horrid revelation.

Silence hung in the air of the study beneath the sea. Basil's eyes locked with the conviction he saw behind the orbs of Theophilus. The shadows danced over the gashes scraped into dead rock.

The sultan had encircled Claudiopolis. That is where Basil would fight. After granting the men with him a day of rest in the walls of Sinope, the Count ordered the march back to the plains of the west, to catch the Turkish army and smash it between the iron of his spears and the stones of the walls. Theophilus rode with him, believing that God had granted his city safety in this present conflict. The occulted words of Tertullian haunted the two riders, adding an angst of apocalypse to their journey.

In a few days of forced march, Basil's army, now numbering almost 3,000 men under arms, nearly all barbarian foreigners, arrived at the outskirts of Claudiopolis. They had traveled across the countryside, shying away from the ancient roads, to keep as far as possible from the eyes of the enemy. The sultan's army had its siege underway, with a handful of catapults hammering the old walls, his men cutting the city off from the farms and life-giving streams of the countryside. The summer heat lay flat and heavy across the plain, bringing a gnawing thirst with it.

Basil secreted the army several miles from the city, behind what hills he could find and forbade them the use of fire. He intended for the Turk to discover them when the first hail of arrows blackened the sky over him, and not a moment before. He and his officers approached the city by foot and spied it from atop a far-off hill. To hide themselves from even keen observers, Basil and his men laid flat on the ground, peering toward the scene of conflict in the dimming sunlight.

The Grand Turk had not come very well prepared, it appeared: he had only three catapults with which to conduct his siege, and no battering ram. His men lay about, not even bothering to attempt to scale the walls of the city. Elsewhere, Constantinople's towering walls were practically unscalable; Claudiopolis had walls merely twenty feet high, easily surmountable by a determined foe. By the number of fires beginning to put up smoke in the twilight, he assumed nearly 9,000 men surrounded the city. While he might not remember the stores in the city's larder, he remembered that the garrison of the city was nowhere near the number now seeking to destroy it.

Basil and his companions retreated to their darkened camp, lit only by starlight. There were many stars in the sky that night. He sat on the warm earth, reporting to the rest of his officers what he saw and what he reckoned ought to be done. The bishop stood over them, listening attentively.

"We are outnumbered perhaps three to one in force of arms. Quality of arms we can assume to be equal: we send barbarians to fight barbarians. They sit on an open plain, where we will lose our tactical advantage once we come out of hiding. The city walls and citadel are in our hands, even if we are cut off from them at the moment, and within we have almost 300 native-born soldiers, perhaps another 1,000 able-bodied men if we impress them to arms," he calmly listed to his commanders.

A junior officer ventured the suggestion, "What if we were to enter the city, which would no doubt open the gates for us, and there consolidate our strength and let the Turk wear himself out on attacking the walls. On certain opportunities we can sally forth, striking at a piece here and a piece there of his army, allowing him no rest. In this heat with no shelter, he will quickly tire, run low on water, and retreat as pestilence takes him. In numbers as great as his, he surely cannot support so great an army in one place for long."

Basil appreciated the assessment from this junior, a promising youth from his own city of

Heraklia. It was not the mere suggestion or boldness to speak in the presence of a superior that Basil approved of from Nicephorus, but the level of detail that went into his thoughts. Perhaps there were some young men who could someday carry the burden of this world.

"Nicephorus, your assessment is good. How much does Claudiopolis have in the way of provisions: food, water, feed for horses?"

Seeing this vulnerability in his plan, Nicephorus nodded in recognition, "I do not know, Count. I would need this before committing my whole army to such a venture."

"Then you have learned how to avoid a potentially fatal mistake, and that will serve you well," smiled Basil in the night. He considered it a primary duty of the old to pass their lessons to the young, perhaps even more valuable in worth than land or possessions. "We would go into what could become a prison for an army, with no certain knowledge of how we, or those already inside, will survive. With our smaller numbers, buttressed though they would be by the defenders inside, we could be held in place by a holding force of the enemy, while he rides away to burn and pillage the surrounding countryside, perhaps destroying other cities in his path. We would be trapped there, lose our freedom of maneuver, and the Turk could continue the war, while we lose the opportunity for a decisive battle."

"Anyone else dare destroy the Turk for me?" he asked, a trace of excited mirth in his voice.

None of the Roman officers answered.

Interrupting the lingering silence, Tughrul, khan and leader of the Cuman horsemen, stood up, his light, pelt-skin robe dropping to its full length. His weathered face framed the words passing his crooked, broken teeth, "We should ride out, gut the enemy, and feast on his corpses."

He always suggested things like that. Basil paid him no mind.

"This is how it looks best to me, my companions: we will launch an ambush on the enemy rear at first light, draw their attention to ourselves, which will be the signal to the garrison to sally forth. Attacking the enemy from the rear, we will confound the Grand Turk with arrows from either side, cast his men into confusion, and allowing the garrison to loot and burn the camp and baggage train of the enemy. We retain freedom of maneuver. If the enemy still has much strength left to him, the garrison resumes its post on the walls, we withdraw for a time, and leave the sultan to his smoldering ruin. If we triumph, we may end the war at a stroke. Are there any questions?"

The dark locks on Nicephorus' brow were shaken aside, as he raised a hand in answer. "Count Argyrus, how do we let the garrison know what to do, and who will lead them in their part?"

Basil answered, "I will. This night I will steal into the city, command the prefect to ready his men for a dawn assault, and return to lead the charge from our front."

"By yourself?" Nicephorus asked with alarm. "Lord, you are far too important to risk being caught!"

"You're right. You do it," Basil responded.

The startled look that gave birth to worry on Nicephorus' face under the night sky brought a laugh to Basil's throat. The look on that smart ass' face! It's moments like these that make being responsible for keeping back the legions of the Antichrist worth it!

107

As Nicephorus looked around to the other officers, chastened by the Count's uncontrollable laughter, the bishop stepped forward. "I will go with you, Count Basil. We will ensure the success of this stealthy enterprise."

Basil calmed himself, took a few deep breaths, and answered the cleric. "No, really, father, I will be fine. Ha, ooh, I can do it myself."

"I will make this journey with you, Count Basil, for this reason: the prefect of the city is a feckless and weak-spined man, even as was my own. Should he fail to be impressed by your authority, I will chasten him and counsel with the bishop to find another to take command, should the prefect fail in his task. Further, the appearance of a man of violence and a man of faith will give heart to the city, making their sally more bold when the time comes."

The surety in the old man's voice aided his cause; as Basil saw on the trek here, he was an agile man for all his elder years. And the bishop may be correct regarding the lack of character of Prefect Demetrius; another detail Basil had overlooked in forming his plan.

"Then let us move now," he agreed, seizing up his cloak. "Nicephorus, should we not return, direct the Cuman khan to launch a fading assault from the west of the city, at twilight. You will press an assault from the enemy's rear and withdraw before you incur one-third casualties. Prepare a harassing campaign, avoiding pitched battles. Your purpose will be to starve and bleed his army with a thousand cuts until he retires from the country. Understood?"

The shock Nicephorus had previously displayed did not resurface. As a lieutenant to the Count, it was his duty to take command should he fall in battle. He knew he lacked Count Argyrus' decades of experience, but he had seen two campaigns before and studied his Caesar and Belisarius. He nodded in recognition of this weighty charge.

The sun was just beginning to break over the horizon. The time for the assault had come.

Neither Basil nor the bishop slept: there was too much to be done to prepare the field of battle and their hoped-for victory. The army stood for a silent prayer service, led by Theophilus giving what

109

blessings he could to the men under the imperial banner, even unto the pagan Cumans.

With the first light approaching over the eastern mountains, the army moved forward. The pagan horsemen rode ahead, showering a hail of arrows to blot out the weak sun onto the horses and riders of the Turk. As the commotion began to stir the enemy camp, the alarm rose up, but Basil and his footmen were too close at hand for the outliers of the encampment to have a chance at survival.

The battle began in earnest. The horns of the Grand Turk sounded, with the core of his army rallying to his standard. His preparations had been lax, and his men now paid the price for his arrogance. Even so, the sultan commanded three times the spears and arrows of the Romans, and they knew how to bring men to woe. His men fought for themselves, for their sultan, their people, and Islam, to which every head will bow. What was this sad Roman force, almost all paid mercenaries, pagans without virtue, and all that could possibly be fielded against their triumphant sultan? With the repeated insults sent to him by that woman of an emperor, this time he came to desolate. He would wreck this land, lay waste its cities, rape their women, and defile their churches. It would be glorious.

An hour passed, and the sun began to climb higher in its ascent. Something had gone horribly wrong.

Basil called for a regrouping of the lines, with his last drive having pushed the Turkish left wing into disarray, but the center holding. The Cumans were earning their pay, keeping the more numerous Turkish horsemen distracted. But where was that damn sally from the walls?! Where were the men of Claudiopolis, as promised by the prefect and bishop of the city?

The battle had gone well so far, but the Turk was finally restoring command over his startled men, and their superior numbers would soon turn the tide. It was too early to tell the casualty numbers, but Basil felt the better of the bloodshed would soon turn away from his advantage.

As the centurions brought discipline to the ranks, the bishop rode to the general, carrying the banner of Rome in his hand. He volunteered to bear the standard of the army, so that another sword would be free to cut at the enemy. He had vowed to never shed blood with his own hands, but he would carry the waving flag of the righteous against any enemy. "Count Basil, what is the plan without the defenders of the city coming to their own rescue?" inquired Theophilus.

Basil did not answer. There was no real alternative. There was no back-up plan. He had that damned Turk's army right here; he could defeat it right now, and be done with it! Where was that worthless nitwit Demetrius and his men? Admittedly, he could sound the retreat, before the Turk launched his full strength at his lines, but damn it! He was about to lose his best chance at actually surviving the war, right here and now.

Theophilus almost heard these thoughts churning inside the heart of the commander. He looked about to survey the lay of the forces, handed the banner over to Nicephorus, and kicked his heels into the ribs of the horse beneath him.

"Father, where are you going?" shouted Nicephorus; Basil just noticed the fleeing bishop.

"To do what must be done!" was all the priest answered.

The ranks reformed in front of Basil too soon for him to follow, and he bade his men remain in their posts. None could help but watch as the old priest galloped toward the city walls. In the fight, the Turk had completely turned his attention away from Claudiopolis, as Basil had anticipated, leaving the priest an emptied camp through which to ride.

As the old man approached the gates, they began to creak open.

From out of the nest of tents and smoking fires of the enemy camp, a band of footmen appeared and gave chase after him.

The bishop and his horse galloped through the gate, disappearing into the city.

The few dozen Turks threw themselves against the wooden gates, a handful wedging themselves inside. A few moments later, one of the enemy stood atop the guard tower and blew a resounding horn that echoed across the plain. They had taken the gatehouse.

In full panic for what was about to happen, Basil called the charge, this time personally plunging into the fray. He had to keep the enemy out here, even if at great loss, to keep them away from the city. If given some time, perhaps the bishop can rally the defenders and join the attack. If not, the city may yet be spared by his sacrifice. There were thousands of people inside those walls, and he meant to stop the Turk from ruining them all.

The sultan now held control of the field. He ordered his infantry in contact with the imperial army to hold their ground; he was going to break the gates. Struggle as he might, Basil could do nothing but fight for his life as he watched the Turkish reserves pour into the open gate, smashing it wide open as it tried to close one last time in vain. It was not long before smoke started to fill the sky.

As the Turkish host marched into the city, the Cuman archers rejoined Basil and his infantry, wheeling around the rear of the seemingly abandoned holding force the sultan ordered to stay in place. Being sliced to ribbons and left in the field by the sultan, the remnants of the Turk's infantry, these being Christian Armenian mercenaries, surrendered. When their commander swore to serve Basil should he spare their lives, it was so.

It was wise of them to do so: the sultan had almost completely drawn himself and his army into the city, and the cries of destruction tore through the air. The ancient city of Claudiopolis was lost.

"Lord!" exclaimed Nicephorus as he rode through the ranks towards Count Basil.

"Lord Basil, what is your order? We hold this ground, but how do we retake the city? The enemy is turning it into a slaughterhouse!" he finished. Nicephorus was correct, besides the newly surrendered Armenians, the Turk had poured everything he had into the city. He had quit the field, decorated with a fresh blossom of wounded and dying, to storm the city.

Basil stared at the white stone walls. He saw the smoke rising over them, the light of the fires burning inside. With the surrender of the Armenians and the assessment of his officers, Basil reckoned that he had 2,000 men left to him, while the sultan razed the city with 5,000 still under arms. The Count performed a grim calculation.

"Sir Nicephorus, you will take your men and seize the enemy catapults. I want you to direct them all at the gatehouse. Bring it down, then continue until you reduce it to impassable rubble. Understood?"

Nicephorus hesitated, confusion troubling his brow. "But how will that save the people inside?"

"It won't," Basil said humorlessly. The color had vanished from his blood-spattered face, and Basil kept his eyes fixed on the walls of the city. "The city is doomed, as are all those inside. We could join them, or we could let their deaths not be in vain. The enemy led himself into a trap. We will block his retreat, sack his camp, and starve him out."

Passion rose inside the young man's heart, yearning for some sort of justice, "But lord, we came here to save these people! They are now at the mercy of the Grand Turk, and he has none for the conquered! We must save them!"

Basil steadied his mount, and finally turned to look at Nicephorus, out of the corner of his eye. "They should have fought when they had the chance." His voice was cold and unyielding.

Nicephorus rocked on his uneasy horse, and he understood his orders. He would trap all these people in a tomb.

A month passed, and the heat of the summer brought misery in its wake. Basil ordered his men to settle in: he besieged the Grand Turk, inside the city he had tried to capture. The irony was not lost on either commander. Unlike the Grand Turk, though, Basil organized and kept a strict watch on the walls and the camp, by day and night. He would not make the same mistake that Suleymanshah had.

No refugees stole over the walls to the safety of the Roman camp. Basil expected all the people inside had been slaughtered, raped, committed suicide, or were being held by the enemy in expectation of selling them later. They were all dead as far as he was concerned. An entire city, and all those from the countryside who had fled into it for their own safety, dead to him.

While the food Basil procured from his own estates had kept his army from starving, the rich victuals they took from the Turkish camp was a delightful feast to his men. In the sultan's tent, he found several barrels of fine French wine, coffee from Ethiopia, and other exotic luxuries; these he gave to his men. He distributed some of the gold and booty they found in the camp to his men, allowing the Armenians to keep what property was rightly theirs, but no pillage taken from the Roman people. He kept aside a portion for the future, to better secure the prosecution of this war. Maybe this battle would end it, and he would have some left to give the refugees something with which to start a new life.

After the first two weeks, the Turk must have exhausted the food supply inside, as he started shouting down messages from the walls. The increasingly unkempt and filthy ruler of the Turks' first offer came that day, saying, "I give you one day to quit the field, lest I crush you when we rejoin you on the field of battle! Leave now, and all the ill-gotten booty you have taken from us. Verily, we will pay you for every head of the faithless Armenians you return to us for execution."

Basil ordered a volley of arrows fired over the wall in response.

The next week, the Turk shouted down from a section of wall not reduced to impassable rubble, looking very haggard, defying Basil, "Quit the field and go your own way, for we wish to leave this place. Should you not do as you are commanded by the Sultan Suleymanshah himself, lord of the Turks, we will kill every last Roman within these walls."

Basil could see him swaying from weakness in the blistering sun. "It's a bluff," thought Basil. Those people are dead already. There is no way the Turk would give slaves food when he was starving.

Over the next week, the sultan and his bodyguard came to the top of the walls every day at noon. Under the bloated sun, they made a show of slitting the throats of a dozen citizens, then kicking them over the wall. The bodies broke in several ways on impact. Basil ordered that they be left there, fearing the Turks' arrows being rained upon those who would go to collect the dead. He suspected the victims were already dead before they were brought to the walls.

On the final day, in desperation, the Turk sallied forth, trying to break out of what was about to become his grave. His men scrambled over the walls and every small way they could find out, starved and weary.

This is what Basil had waited for. As the thousands of ruined Turks made it over the stones, the Cumans flung arrow after arrow at their victims, picking them off like rats fleeing a hole. Those that made it past the horsemen Basil's infantry fell upon, hacking them down as they feebly fought for their lives.

Pulling his spear from the young Turk's skull, he felt vindicated. An army he could not defeat on the field, he ruined through audacity, starvation, and sheer inhumanity. He chose to risk it all in one decisive battle, and it paid off. There was a price, and he would someday pay his portion.

As Basil looked up, his eyes caught a rapid glint moving in the distance. He saw a lone rider flying to the south, the colors of the sultan on his back. The war can end here, he knew. Grabbing the reigns of his horse, Basil mounted, riding in hot pursuit. He had no precious time to waste calling for reinforcements: he could kill this man himself.

The gap began to close, Basil's fresh strength swiftly overcoming the sultan's tired steed.

The sultan looked back in time to see Basil hefting his heavy spear and to pull his horse out of the path of the hurled javelin.

The sultan pulled his exhausted horse to a halt, both faces blistered with thirst and cracked from the heat. He drew his long, glimmering sword in the hazy light of the day. Count Basil slowed his horse from its gallop, turning to face the Grand Turk.

"You are as audacious as you are cruel to your own people, I see," taunted the sultan. Beaten, tired, and cornered he no doubt was; willing to surrender, the Turk was too proud and overweening to ever be. "Did you decide you want to have the blood of everything that ever lived in those walls on your hands?"

Basil pulled his sword and stalked toward the enemy, taunting Suleymanshah, "Did your boy not tell you? Your sweet, young boy you tried to offer me in the beginning of all this? I have never lost a battle with your filthy kind. I see you are no better than the mongrels that brought you forth. It's sad to see what passes for a king amongst the infidels."

Suleymanshah leered a smile and protested, "It did not have to be like this at all, Count Basil. Even now, all you have to do is bow before me, and all will be forgiven. Just bow to me and profess that there is no god but Allah, and that Mohammed is his prophet, and all this suffering can end. You will be the greatest of my generals! Accept this gift, turn away from that pathetic emperor of yours. I offer this to you for I am most merciful, most kind."

Basil beheld the image of Muslim piety before him: filthy, bedraggled, rich silks and garments, caked with old blood. He answered, "I saw your mercy. I fed those you drove from their homes, though I prayed for those you caught. I protect those you would sell into slavery," he parried a strike from the sultan's blade. "I honor God and His Son, and hold sacred the woman who nurtured Him. You defile them all, and for what?"

Suleymanshah grinned. "You know, to be honest, I was glad when that coward that commands your faithful declared war on me to his German cousins. I am a man of ambition, Basil, a man of greatness. I couldn't find an excuse to attack anymore of my own faithful, and the Crusaders were too far away, but then he gave me the answer, clear as day: I am to conquer the Empire of Rome. How do you like that: the Sultan who became Caesar? You like that?" he chuckled, smiling broadly.

Basil led in furiously with a slash. The sultan parried, returning the strike. The two began striking in earnest, both men hungry for the blood of the other.

As the weakness of the sultan began to tell, an arrow whizzed between them, planting into the ground. Both men stopped and looked at it, and it was followed by several more. They looked around, catching sight of their own horse archers approaching from both the north and the south. The two men circled about each other one more time.

Basil prepared for a last charge, when a bolt from the sky struck his sword, knocking it from his hand.

The sultan smiled before he began to ride away, leaving his opponent with these words: "You have fought well, but I will return. Before I am done, I will rape your Virgin and make your home a fiery ruin, in your honor. Allah be with you, dear Basil!"

As a fresh volley of arrows came hurling toward him from the sky, Basil turned and rode back to his men in sheer frustration. One on one, he knew he could slay the sultan; the arrival of the horsemen was most unwelcome. And he knew the sultan intended to keep his promises.

"None are to enter the city until I give the order," Basil stated flatly to his officers. The army had devastated the weakened Turks, taking a few as prisoners and slaying the rest. The officers had waited for the Count's instructions regarding what remained of Claudiopolis, for fear of a trap waiting on the other side.

This had been his decision. "I will reconnoiter the city, and when I declare it so, the men may enter."

"Who will you take with you, lord?" asked Nicephorus.

"No one. I go alone," he finished. Riding alone to the base of the walls, he dismounted, approaching the rubble that had been the gate. As his men watched in silence, he scaled the broken stones into the city.

Standing atop the stones, he looked down the streets before him for lurking enemy or starving citizens. He saw a trail of smoke being moved by the southerly wind, past the blasted buildings. He heard nothing inside the city.

Walking down, he entered the ghost town. By the inside of the gate, there were stacks of freshly dead Turks, arrows protruding from their eyes, limbs, and breasts. A few paces away, he found the rotten defenders, those who had tried to close the gate a month ago, when it was already too late. He knew the putrid smell would only get worse the further he went.

He found the city an abattoir. Charred buildings, ruined churches. Down every avenue, he saw the protruding bones of the city, the timbers, the pillars, broken and jagged, out of their proper place. The city was quiet, save when he heard the cawing of distant carrion crows, come to feast on his people. In the lanes of the horse track, the hippodrome where all the people came to enjoy festivals and watch entertaining feats of charioteering, he found the ground covered by stacked bodies, rotten and burned by the sun. Much of the flesh had turned black, the native Romans indistinguishable from the invaders, and the flies made a feast in this place.

At long last, he came to the holy see of the city of Claudius, the church that was the heart of faith in the city. The door fell off the hinges when he pushed it open, giving a great noise to resound upon the dead altar. The gold mosaics on the wall, which once depicted God and His angels, were hacked to pieces, lying broken on the floor. To the Turk, the base gold that made up the miracle of craftsmanship and inspiration was worth far more than the beauty and light it brought to mankind.

As he stalked further inward, he saw his lost friend, suspended from the bronze chandelier, strung up by his feet.

"Here you are, Theophilus," he thought. He knew it to be his brave friend, as he knew the face on the flayed skin he found on the floor beneath the blackened skeleton.

It was his decision that made this happen. Theophilus had bought Rome this victory.

Magnaura Palace, night of the 16th of July, 1203

Emperor Alexius the Third decided it was time to be Emperor of All the Romans somewhere else. His nobles, the ones that would actually fight at any rate, spat at him and abandoned him in disgust. The Catholic army had made it to shore outside of the City, a few months ago, bringing his little bastard nephew with them. To Emperor Alexius' relief, the people and the Court had not cared, no matter how much the Crusaders paraded him around outside the walls.

The Catholics almost took those walls a couple of times, but had been beaten back. This wasn't because of Alexius' brave leadership or inspired military defenses; this was because of his men, laughing at the ridiculously outnumbered Crusaders, laying siege to at most a few yards of a wall miles long. While he stayed chafing with angst inside the walls, his ministers and nobles kept pressing him, "When will we attack? When will we drive them out? Why are these Franks still here?" Finally, he gave in, and ordered all the mercenaries available to be rounded up.

Earlier today, 30,000 of the cruelest men money could buy were assembled in front of the Church of Hagia Sophia, facing the massive colosseum called the Hippodrome. From high in the Imperial Box, the Emperor saw an ocean of men flying banners from the unknown corners of the world, gibbering in a thousand mongrel tongues. He was terrified: all this had been inside his City this whole time? He had precious few Romans to die for him; had these barbarians not known that? Did they not smell the rot at the heart of the Apple of the World?

No matter: they would be unleashed on the Christians outside the gates, who did know the frailty of the Empire. He would crush these vital men, butcher them for the audacity to unseat this Usurper!

So he quietly told his Master of the Horse to march them to the field of battle, and the horns sounded. The City shook with the din of these brutes, and they filled the avenues with their marching. The citizens took shelter inside their homes as the horde passed them by, hoping the animals would stay on their tethers.

Alexius III followed after them, carried on his litter. He surmounted the walls, overlooking the small Crusader camp on the fields below. As the great gate opened, the wealth of tyrants poured out, like a river about to devour a forest. The Master of the Horse asked for the command to strike.

The Emperor hesitated. Fear took him. He stared at what threatened him and what else he saw before him. He had seen the wealth and privilege Isaac had enjoyed, and had his own fill. He saw the courtiers and commoners alike bow to him, speak to him as a God! Why should his younger brother have that?! Why not he, who had suffered so much in prisons across the East, before he was rescued?

Isaac had gone on a hunting trip when Alexius' bought men declared him Caesar. Alexius ordered his brother hunted down, thrown in shackles, and blinded with white-hot irons. Now he would be Emperor! People would bow before him!

Never mind that he knew nothing of being a ruler and lacked any of the character to be an Emperor. The Bulgars, the Germans, the Turks, they all could smell his weakness, knew that he feared being tested, so they robbed his people, stole his money, raped his women, and killed his men.

And he wanted to talk. Diplomacy was the answer, he thought, because no one got hurt: more importantly, he did not get hurt. He got to sit in his palace, make a big show of himself to men who wanted everything he had, and then cravenly beg that they only take 1,000 pounds of gold, instead of 5,000. They took his money, left, and then took everything else they could get their hands on, until men like Basil stopped them.

Now that Alexius had to fight, he could not. He turned. He walked away.

For four hours, his general tried to get him to give the order, but he would not. He stood in his throne room, staring out the window at the sea. The Emperor would not utter a word.

The prefect of Constantinople came to ask the Master of the Horse why there was no clash of steel resounding in the air. When he heard of the failing of the Emperor, he ordered the Master of the Horse to stand the men down. No one would die for that man.

No matter to Alexius, though. When he heard the prefect had taken control, he was relieved. And ready to leave. He ordered Menelik and his daughter to gather all the money they could fit on a boat, and get ready to leave. They obeyed with enthusiasm.

As Alexius passed through the mother-of-pearl archway, he knew he had everything he needed ready to sail. Imposing manservant? Yes. The daughter he actually liked? Yes. Enough gold to choke an elephant? Yes. Nagging, sagging wife? She always liked the palace, better to just leave her here.

Alexius was inspecting the last parcel of treasures in his arms when he was startled. A few paces down the pier stood a man dressed in black, with a white shirt underneath. He was pale, raven-haired, and wearing a suit of the most foreign cut. The night air seemed too quiet: only the muted sound of the lapping waters reaching Alexius' ears.

"What do you want? My soldiers will be here in a moment, I suggest you leave," the retreating Emperor said defensively.

The man grinned. "Scream if you want. I don't think they'll come," he man muttered, his hands concealed in his pockets.

Alexius had chosen the favorites who obeyed him most slavishly to come with him, as he enjoyed being the master. This man clearly had none.

The Emperor felt his skin turn cold. Angelus pulled his wealth closer to him, as if to hide it, as if it could warm him. "What do you want?"

"Nothing. Just to watch."

"I'm afraid I don't understand," Alexius solicited, unsure and unnerved by this person he had never seen before. A clammy sweat broke out on his skin. Alexius had all the strength and resolve of a coward fleeing the scene of his shame, and still he was paralyzed by the stranger's mere gaze.

The man in black sauntered a few steps closer, then stood still.

The soldiers on the boat at the end of the pier continued to work, tying ropes, and packing the goods away, unaware of anything amiss.

"Do you mean to rob me?" Alexius asked, shrinking away. "GUARDS!" he shouted.

The soldiers stopped to listen to Menelik give them instructions on how to secure the rigging.

"I told you they wouldn't listen," spoke the ageless man as he stepped forward again.

"Are you going to kill me?" he asked, his throat dry as a bone in the desert.

The man took the last few steps forward, eliminating the safe distance between him and the disgraced apostle. The cold man smelled of honeyed perfume. It was on the edge of sickly and sweet, and it filled Alexius' nostrils.

His eyes flashed from the plunder in the Emperor's hands to his fearful eyes.

"No. You don't die today. I wanted to thank you. Because you were such an ungrateful little shit, I get to come home."

In his last act as Emperor, Alexius pursed his lips and looked in fear on this man's face.

The man moved closer, to whisper in his ear. Alexius trembled underneath his ruby and gold encrusted robes. "Take comfort, Alexius. I once put it to the man, 'That if anyone murder a person, it would be as if he murdered the whole people. And if anyone saved a life, it would be as if he saved the whole world.' Now, I don't know how the math works out for you, but let that comfort you, as you wait for me."

Constantinople, 17th of July, 1203

"My prince, the keys to the kingdom," growled Doge Dandolo, grinning triumphantly as he handed the tarnished key to young Alexius.

Young Alexius Angelus was beside himself with the glory of the day: just last twilight, his uncle Alexius III had marched an army of giants to menace the outnumbered Crusader camp, and now there was no Emperor Alexius III on the throne!

When Count Geoffrey de Villehardouin had failed to deliver either the 40,000 promised Crusaders or the kingly sum to pay Venice for the hundred warships his republic had dedicated all their efforts to building and manning for an entire year, prince Alexius' offer seemed not only favorable, but also necessary to save Venice from ruin. It also saved the Crusaders from being sold into slavery by a righteously furious Doge.

After sacking a rival city-state to help pay off the Crusade's enormous debt, Dandolo and Geoffrey managed to inspire or brow-beat most of the knights to help overthrow Alexius III and liberate the blinded

Isaac from captivity. Some refused to attack their fellow Christians and left.

Those that stayed sailed to Constantinople and risked everything in this family squabble. Try as they might, the walls of the City proved impenetrable, and supplies were running low. Some of the knights had to raid for the food the Roman forces were slowly starving them of. Then Emperor Alexius III marshaled an ocean of mercenaries, the brutal flowering of a hundred nations, and rode behind them to the Crusader camp. Dandolo remained with young Alexius and the fleet, blockading the walls; Geoffrey and the knights were trapped on land, facing annihilation.

Death or victory their only options, the army rallied and stood defiant against the violent wealth of the East. These mercenaries had been paid to take the field on behalf of the Usurper; these knights had spent all of their fortunes to stand on this ground. Shouting defiantly beside their standards, they faced the horde for four hours.

Then it slowly retreated. Emperor Alexius III had called the retreat. That night, he silently packed as much money as he could take and slipped out the gate.

The next day, the prefect of the city sent for counsel with the Doge and prince Alexius. They were welcomed into the City; the soldiers were not. It took three days for the Doge and de Villehardouin to stop their men from looting and burning.

Prince Alexius stared at the key in disbelief. Dandolo cleared his throat, causing the prince to fumble at the lock. Geoffrey de Villehardouin stood behind the old man, smiling in his gleaming armor. He was still confused by the morality of his triumph: in the noble, Christian Crusade he had organized, they had so far sacked one, now two Christian cities, spilling Christian blood, in the effort to pay off their Christian Venetian brethren. How many more of the faithful would he have to make bleed before he could confront the infidel?

The smell of sea air greeted Alexius, as he shed torchlight into the seaside prison of his father. He trembled as he entered the grotto, shouting, "Father, your son has returned! You are free!"

A wasted, withered man turned to look at him, the burned, blackened holes that were his eyes searching in the dark grotto. "My son?" he croaked weakly. "Is it you?"

"YES, FATHER!" he proclaimed, rushing to embrace Isaac. He clutched the deposed man he had despaired of ever seeing again in this lifetime. The scant strength in Isaac flowed to grip his son in turn.

"You are restored, Emperor Isaac II. This holy Crusade has chased away the traitor who did this to you. God be praised!" beamed Alexius, his whole body shivering with the joy of saving the life of the man who gave him his.

"Who has worked this miracle, my son?" asked Isaac, warily.

The tone did not yet alarm Alexius, who responded enthusiastically, "Doge Enrico Dandolo of Venice, father, and the Pope's own army of Christian warriors, gathered by Count Geoffrey de Villehardouin! These men have restored us!"

"Ah," muttered Isaac, as he pulled away from his son. The old man turned on his marble stump, his chains rattling. Facing the nocturnal sea, he asked, "And what price did they ask?"

"I promised them land to support 500 knights, 10,000 talents of gold, and the might of all the Roman Empire to march in their Crusade."

Isaac stared off, morose.

"Father, you are free now! The Empire is yours once more! Why are you not overjoyed by this?" inquired his worried son.

"We don't have it."

"Surely you jest! The palaces alone could pay for all of –"

"We don't have it," Isaac interrupted. "The treasury has been empty for a long time. We don't even have the land to give them."

As Alexius' triumph quickly started to sour, he fought to keep it. "Father, we can raise the money somehow. Together, we can retake the land from the Turks for the knights," he finished, defeat flavoring his tone.

Isaac knew a Devil's bargain when he heard it. He had prayed for an end to his misery, assuming that meant death. This might be worse.

"Very well, my young Emperor Alexius the Fourth. Take me to our thrones."

Kiev, 10th of September, 1203

It was only September, but Dukas already felt the bite of Mother Winter descending on the steppes of the north. He had traveled from court to court in this flat land, riddled with rivers and barbarians. It was sometimes hard to tell the Christians from the pagans. He traveled armed and searched for further arms to hire, but so far had received none.

He had only one companion left with him; his porter had died of the plague last month. Dukas' remaining companion was Constantine Lascaris, who had been an acquaintance before the incident where his father Manuel slapped sense into Dukas. However, the two men had grown closer due to the ties of patriotism that they found in common and their shared struggles. Watching the two noblemen trying to pay their own way and see to their own needs, without a staff of servants, would be amusing to an outside observer, but the pair was almost proud of what they were learning of themselves and how the world works with no safety net.

The limitless blue sky stretched above them, and the pair began their ascent up the low steps rising to the stone hall of the prince of this place. He hoped for better fortune here: Prince Roman Mstislavich had married Princess Anna, a niece of Isaac II. He was tied to the Empire and a champion of the Orthodox Church, so perhaps he would help drive back the Turk from dominion over the long-suffering Christians of the East.

The clean-cut, white stone walls of the palace were guarded by two rough, pelt-clad men holding gruesome axes on their shoulders. Dukas noted the lack of discipline and decorum on the part of the guardsmen, but he did not doubt their ability. They came from a culture of violence that prized strength, not soft wit or guile. These men hesitated not in gutting either the beast that would become their dinner or the men who stood against them. This land was ruled by a chorus of princes, men who seized land and held it against all comers. There was something appealing about this to Dukas, a kind of honesty. Fortune, faith, and right and wrong were worth fighting for, and these men knew that.

Alexius and Constantine made their introductions to the guards, who showed them in, as their visit had been expected. The interior of the castle was as stark white as the exterior, with only sparse decoration to ornament the walls. There was no crimson carpet or jade-covered mosaics depicting the prince as a Christian version of Hercules. There were sconces on the walls, being stocked by a servant with fresh torches to light the coming night.

At the end of the hall, a blue and scarlet robed short man awaited them in front a black, iron-reinforced wooden door, his eyes narrowed, piercing the supplicants. "Welcome to the court of Volhynia, under the faithful watch of Prince Roman the Great," said the man, turning over a silver key in his hands. "I am Dmitri Vladimirovich, advisor of the Great Prince. You are the Roman delegation then, I presume?"

Dukas spoke first, "Greetings to our brothers in the faith of Christ, Master Vladimirovich. I am Alexius Dukas, and this is Constantine Lascaris, both honored members of the Court of Constantinople, heir to the legacies of Caesar and Christ. We come on behalf of the Empire to discuss the matters of war with the Grand Turk, as our letter promised."

Dmitri eyed them suspiciously. "Only two from the Court of the Center of the World? Why, even the Poles send larger delegations to make entreaties with the Prince."

Dukas explained, "We come on a mission of diplomacy in our capacities as citizens of the Empire, not on the Emperor's request. Your countrymen have my condolences, as our escort discovered that the plague still haunts this land."

"Ah, indeed it does," said Dmitri with understanding. "Before we enter into the presence of the Great Prince, make your business clear. I know you have been searching for mercenaries in these lands. Your coin is ample, and your name has prestige." Dmitri eyed Dukas coldly. "I am aware that a Dukas has sat on the Gloried Throne of the Caesars before. If you intend on embroiling us in a fool-hardy attempt for the Crown, we have no interest. There are quite enough enemies of the True Faith and my prince in these lands without stirring up your meddlesome kind."

Dukas' prodigious eye-brows furrowed in spite, but he was cut off as Lascaris held up a hand to stop his torrent of expletives. Constantine was well-aware that Dukas had rightfully earned the nickname "The Sullen", because it did not take much to provoke a down-trodden ridicule from the young noble. Rather, Constantine smiled his pearly white teeth from under his black beard and answered for his friend.

"Master Dmitri, our reputation as Romans precedes us! Why, Alexius, it seems that the chief export of our native land is merely ill-words of the foul deeds we commit against each other. Master Vladimirovich, you have the point in that part of the negotiations, and I will offer no contest. However, it may please you to know we are here to ask assistance against the Grand Turk, who is even now at war with a man of steady Christian virtue and all the Faithful, who are enslaved by his vices. While our Emperor started a war He had no means to win, He did command a man very dear to us and all the bishops of our Empire to fight it for Him. We suspect that the Emperor did this in bad faith, so rather than let a good man die and the Holy Church be further desecrated, we have come to this court. Your prince is mighty and true in defense of the Church, no doubt aided by your wise hand, and can surely not turn away faithful supplicants," Constantine punctuated with a jingle of coin at his waist.

"Well, you have spoken most persuasively," smiled Dmitri, his eyes falling to the purse. He extended his hand to Constantine, saying, "Christian charity is a beautiful thing, and the good prince is most charitable. One day, he dreams to march against the Muslims, instead of the same droll pagans he has so often vanquished."

Constantine slipped the small velvet bag into the advisor's palm.

Dmitri's smile went back into hiding, as he spoke, concluding, "Allow me to inform the Prince of your request, and in due time, call you for audience. Wait here," he stopped disinterestedly, as he walked down the hallway, away from the iron-bound oak door leading to the Prince's hall.

Dukas seethed. "You are the junior partner in this venture, I could speak for myself."

"Because you were getting along so well with the gatekeeper as it was," retorted Constantine.

Dukas glared at Lascaris.

Constantine continued, "Peace be upon you, Alexius. You don't want the Prince to see that warm face of yours like that, do you?"

Dukas soaked in his repressed, but not hidden, vitriol. The sunnier dispositioned Lascaris, for whom life held limitless opportunities if you were willing to find and follow them, let him enjoy his glower.

The hardwood doors began to open on their groaning hinges, and the warmth of fire flowed out of the hall into the chilled entryway. Sitting on the throne was a tall ox of a man, relaxed in his power. He was wearing clean white cloth, not the heavy garments typical for these cold lands. On his brow rested a simple gold circlet, with a red stone at its center. His style was plain compared to the Court of Constantinople, and more honest. This man proved his importance to any who beheld him, without draping himself with jewels and silks.

The white stone floor was devoid of any decoration, the walls unadorned with ivory carvings that cost a hundred elephants their lives. The room was small, perhaps only a quarter the size of the Emperor's Court. As Dukas and Lascaris entered, the door was closed behind them, saving the heat from the roaring fireplaces as a precious creature comfort against the devouring winds. Seated at long tables were a dozen men, warriors, perhaps the Prince's favorites by the look of them. They ate of their meat and drank heartily, unconcerned with the Greeks' entrance, or the audience about to occur.

The enthroned man rose, calling out in a bear of a voice, "Welcome, Romans from your far-country! Welcome to my court. I am Prince Roman Mstislavich. I have won four crowns, and I will yet gain more if God wills it. Please, be at home in my company! There is ample fodder for you at my table," he finished, resuming his seat.

"Okay, this is too much," thought Dukas. He had been to three of these Norsemen's courts so far, and none of them knew how to properly occupy the throne yet. They had barely any servants about to tend them or their guests, certainly no eunuchs; this one actually has mere knights EATING IN HIS THRONE ROOM; only one had used a herald to announce Dukas and Lascaris' arrival; and this one actually rose when his guests entered the court. Amateurs!

At least this one spoke Greek.

Lascaris waited for too long to let Dukas speak, and the Prince saw the sullen man's thoughts racing about his mind. "What troubles do you bring before me, Alexius Dukas? I knew you wanted swords for your cause, but this is the part where you speak of that, instead of looking at the floor in wrath," interjected the Prince.

Dukas' eyes flashed up at the Prince, and spat out, "It's disgust, Your Highness."

Prince Roman countered, "Please, my name is Roman. We are all nobles here, and all are equal before Christ."

Did this man lack all decorum! "Prince Roman, I have traveled some time looking for soldiers in this backward land, and all I've beheld is squalor, meanness, and a lack of any dignity in those who claim noble blood. Even the Bulgars ape the ways of high courts, but I don't even see a pretension of it here!" fumed Dukas.

Lascaris was shocked by the brazen insults hurled by his companion and took him by the right arm, pulling him back toward the door. "Please beg my most humble apologies, Roman! My friend feels like he has a fever!" Dukas' annoyance did not abate, but he did not resist his friend's pull.

Roman assessed Dukas with concern and some puzzlement. Before Constantine could open the door to ensure their retreat, he called, concern in his voice, "Wait, Lascaris. Sir Dukas, what is the cause of this outburst? You have traveled so far for my or any of my countrymen's succor, yet now you spew vitriol at one who invited you to his table. If you think so low of us, why did you step into our muck?"

Dukas breathed hard, not knowing if he wanted to smash his fist into the dining tables or scream out his agitation. One of the knights appeared to Alexius' left, startling him from his reverie. The bearded, burly man wrapped in a bear cloak did not smile or speak: he handed Dukas a stein of sweet-smelling beer, then returned to his dinner.

"Well?" requested Roman.

Dukas hesitated, his mouth opening then closing in confusion. "How embarrassing," he thought to himself, "I come seeking the aid of these barbarians, then I set loose my revulsion at their ways." What bothered him most, though, was he didn't really think it was the barbarians that disgusted him.

He looked up from the beer to the Prince. "Lord Roman, what I said is true, if spoken by a callow, worthless shit. I hope you can judge it to be false words in my case. I'm sorry, Roman; I'm more disgusted by myself and my people. Strangers in these lands, we have been given hospitality from all our hosts, the most sincere at this very court. The wealth of our home is greater than this entire land, but it is full of weak, false men, more akin to boys and hysterical women than true men. Certainly, this is a land full of strife, but there is honesty there: each of you lords can rest comfortably in your beds, knowing your death will come in battle, rather than poison by your own wife or a pillow from a castrati in your sleep."

He stopped to sip the drink he remembered was in his hand. It was strong and sweet, new and very exciting. He handed it to Constantine, to share this discovery. He continued, walking toward the Prince, "For whatever faults there may be here, I see you supping with your men, and I know that each of you gamble your lives with your wars and decisions. Your princedom is your life, not something you abuse and use like a wretch. Unlike my Emperor, you do not send good men to their deaths while you whittle away your life behind the safety of others' lives."

Roman listened, turning over Alexius' words in his mind. "I appreciate the nobility of spirit and manliness you find in our court. You have a sharp eye to see that so quickly, and I assure you, you see correctly. However, you have given me pause for trouble. You are emissaries of the true Roman Empire, the very Court of God's Man on Earth. You come to ask for my arms to help defend it, yet I doubt you find in it anything worth saving! Is this true, Sir Dukas? Have you come all this way and suffered so much for something you despise?"

Constantine did not wait to speak this time. "My friend is nicknamed 'The Sullen' in our tongue for a reason, I assure you. The Roman Empire is –"

"I did not ask you to defend your homeland, fair Constantine, thank you. This is the man who has come before me. I need to know what feelings lie in his heart," asserted the Prince.

Dukas considered these words. He grabbed the mug back, taking a heady swig of the brew. He turned to face the fireplace, filled with red and gold flames, casting the heat of its base substance on the people here assembled. Was there nothing of worth left to him in the Empire Caesar built?

There was much rot. Sure, the Empire had been ravaged because of the iniquity and incompetence of many Emperors before and been able to fight its way back to greater glories. But where were the men who would lead the charge?

When Dukas looked around, he saw only vipers too cowardly to strike at the Empire's enemies without, but advantaged enough to devour the few inside trying to keep it going. Then, the sparking logs reminded him. "Roman, have you ever seen the City at sunset?" he asked, still staring into the fire.

Roman shook his head. "I have not had the pleasure. Someday I will pilgrimage to Its Holy Places, but my crown needs me here."

Dukas' eyes turned to the Prince, a distant look in them. "If one stands on the sea, or across the strait, he will behold a wonder the ancients could never fabricate. The spires of the palaces, the dome of the Hagia Sophia, the glittering of the sun's gold on the rippling waters. It's a beauty without equal." He turned to face Roman full-on.

"Yes, my lord, there is some good left there. The women still guard their virtue, for the most part. Even in parts of the Empire still lost, Romans join their monasteries and dedicate their lives fully to God. The ancient sages are still taught, and their wisdom spread to almost all the citizens of the City. I remember," he chuckled, "a tale of a visiting Latin priest, who complained that he could not even buy a loaf of bread without the baker attempting to debate theology with him!

"But these are not the people at the helm of the state, Roman," he grew grim. "There is good in the commoners, yes, but they live under heel to the rotten aristocracy. Our Emperor gained His Throne only by betraying His Own Brother, but because He sits on the Throne, He is to be considered the Equal of the Apostles, God's Viceroy on Earth. And what did our true and virtuous legion of nobility do? We stood by and did nothing while He condemned His Innocent

Brother to suffering. His Younger Brother was not a gem, but he was not a monster."

Roman nodded in understanding. However, he was never content to just understand. "And what are you doing about it, Alexius? What are you doing about this injustice that oppresses your land?" he finished, sweeping his left arm wide.

"I have left the comfort of my Empire, the safety of my home, and come to you, seeking your aid in defending it."

He nodded once more, responding, "You have sought good and true men to fight for your cause, this is true. But what about your own men? Is it not true, that if your Empire has no good men left in It, that God will visit His Judgement upon It? I could ride forth with all my men to ravage the Turk, which I hope to someday do, but of what use is that if I only hand it over to debased and corrupt men who thank me for my Christian charity and then dishonor the God I serve?"

Dukas shook his head in objection, as he swallowed more of the brew. Clearing his throat, he fought back, "But there are good men there, good Roman. There is one, Count Basil Argyrus, who keeps peace in his lands, and rode forth without complaint to fight the Turk. My friend in the Court, Nicetas Choniates, brother to the Bishop of Athens, works behind the scenes to foil the plots of those scoundrels that thrive in the rotten heart of the Court."

Gesturing to his right, Dukas said, "The Lascaris family is filled with good and wise men. It was Constantine's father that advised I head North in search of men who yet had strength in their hearts to counter the rapacity of the Grand Turk. Constantine has braved and survived plague to come with me thence, and there are many more in the Empire."

Roman nodded, rising once more from his simple wooden throne. He walked deliberately down the dais, until he came face to face with Dukas. "And what are you doing about it?"

Dukas looked the Prince in the eyes. Here was a man who had gained his crown with his own hand. His deeds had brought low hordes of pagans, and his deeds of piety brought the adoration of even the Patriarch of Constantinople. Dukas knew what he would do.

155

"I will restore honor to the Empire, fair Roman."

The Prince smirked assuredly. "How will you bring It that honor, Alexius?"

"I will make the Emperor conduct Himself as He should, as an heir to Caesar and follower of Christ. If any of His Advisors counsel cowardice or treachery in His Heart, my friends and I will bring them low through any means necessary. Or, Devil take Him, I will take His Place!" roared Dukas.

A robust twinkle sparkled in Roman's eye. He raised a cup in toast, knocking it against Dukas'. "Spoken like a king among men! You have shown me that there is yet still strength left in the heart of old Rome."

Roman gestured for the visitors to sit at his table with him, as he continued the conversation. "I have received word that the Pope wishes to speak to me concerning the error of my ways. My advisor tells me, sometime soon, a delegation may arrive here to ask me to switch my allegiance to him, rather than his brother, the Patriarch in the City. I believe I know what I will tell him."

Dukas felt game, asking, "And what will you tell these merchants of blessings?"

Roman gave him a sly grin, "I will look at his emissary and say to him words I now give to you," as he reached for and drew his sword. "Say: 'Is the Pope's sword similar to mine? So long as I carry my own, I need no other.' Gentlemen, my faith has made me strong, and that faith I drew from the rightly guided. I have no need to win the favor of the Pope or other courts by trading away that which is most dear to my heart."

These words were not lost on the Greeks.

"As you now understand my quality, I can offer you men. Ride forth from here in a week, and you will have 3,000 men with which to battle the Turk, in our common cause. I even have a commander I can spare you. But for your own struggle, that for the heart of your Empire, find your own sword. Dukas, he who lives by his own sword, lives or dies by it. Without the true sword of the Caesar's, your Empire will not stand another day."

Dukas would find that sword.

Phrygian Mountains, 16th of December, 1203

Word reached Basil in the East of the Catholic invasion. The Sultan of Iconium had marched upon hearing the declaration of war by Emperor Alexius III and began ravaging his way towards Bithynia. His objective: burn the lands and enslave the people of the general ordered against him. With no time to spare, Basil rode out with what troops were ready, and without the host being assembled in the City for him by his friend Dukas. If the sultan ruined this man, then none of the Emperor's other men would accept the task of standing against him again.

That had been the sultan's plan, anyway. After Basil smashed the Turkish army at Claudiopolis, the sultan barely escaped with his life, vowing revenge. Several months later, the Grand Turk marched again, this time bringing all forces under his dominion to the field. He would massacre every Roman he found and personally torture their leader until he begged for death. Every head will bow.

Basil marched his 2,000 men against the Turk's 10,000, and managed to bottle his foe up in the mountains through ruse and maneuver. He could not risk a pitched battle: he was outnumbered, and mercenaries break and run too quickly. He and the Grand Turk ambushed and cornered each other in defiles and gorges through the winter, in the mountains and passes. Snow-choked lakes felt steaming blood rain down on them.

Basil liberated a camp of villagers from the Muslim slave-chattels. The next village was simply slaughtered, rather than taken to the slaver's market.

In a raid on Christmas day, the Turk was lying in wait. Basil's horse was shot out from under him, and his closest companions, true Romans all, were brutally cut down. With an arrow in his leg, he prepared to make his end. In a complete surprise, the heathen Cuman mercenaries broke through the Turkish mob, pulled his bleeding body up, and fled the field.

Fortified at the head of the gorge barring the way to the plains of Bithynia, the Count surveyed his forces. 1,000 men were left to him, and his money and food were almost gone. Reinforcements had not come: he conscripted every man strong enough to heft a spear, and spent all the wealth his forefathers had left him to keep them alive. The Turk had been battered, but not wearied.

The snow was storming down the cliffs, when Basil spotted riders on the western horizon. Awaiting word from his sentries, he only prayed that the Turk had not found a way around.

Moments later, he relaxed: the horns had not been sounded, and the men did not flee. If it was the Turk, at least they could all be massacred in peace and quiet. Basil always hoped for a violent death, free of the panic and confusion of not knowing why one is dying he found so distasteful.

As the riders came into sight, he beheld the double-headed eagle on the red banner of the Empire. He breathed relief when he saw Alexius Dukas riding this way, even if cheer did not overtake him.

"Basil, my friend," saluted Dukas, as he dismounted and handed his reins to a servant. He flung aside his fur-lined cloak, as he embraced the Count. "You look as bleak as the passes we crossed. How goes the reconquest of Asia?"

"The Turk is an implacable foe. The cost has been great, but we yet draw breath. These heathens have been true warriors," Basil finished morosely, as he limped into his tent. Taking a seat, he gestured to a hard heel of bread, saying, "Let me offer you our bounty."

Eyeing the cold, empty insides of the tent, Dukas responded, "Then the City's calamity is your gain." Breaking a crumb from the wonting loaf, he continued, "Has word of the invasion reached this far?"

Numb from cold and atrocity, Basil shrugged unconcernedly. That Damned City. So far away, yet the cause of all his troubles. Given an impossible war, no money, no reinforcements, and an overwhelming adversary, the Emperor sent him out here to die. The Turk laughed at him, once riding forth to offer him a place in his infernal court. Sometimes he thought of throwing in with the Turk. The life of a pagan warlord was so easy: just kill your enemies, make slaves of the women you desire, and be done with it! He would have said yes. If he could ever deny the love of Christ, or the memory of Irene.

Taken aback by the despair in his once hale and powerful friend, Dukas pressed on. "I have brought for you mercenaries, gold, and food. I bring a commander from Crete to give you rest. The Empire needs you now, Basil."

Swelling with rage, Basil snapped out loud. "How dare Rome ask more of me now! Is it not enough that my people are slaughtered, my lands laid to waste, my life almost surrendered, my mongrel soldiers paid to die in the place of Romans not worthy of the name?! How dare the Emperor ask this of me in this Hell of exile!"

Raising his palms in innocence, Dukas retorted, "My friend, Alexius III is no longer on the throne: he fled with all he could carry to the sea. The Catholic army restored Isaac II to the Throne, and His Son with Him. They have sold us all and our Church to the Pope for their thirty shekels of silver."

The Count took all this in, cursing the Angelus family and the wastrels of men they made. Three traitorous emperors they had produced, with each devastating the legacies of Caesar, Constantine, and Christ, as if in some perverse competition. "Curse them all," he thought.

"So what does it dare ask of me?"

"The Empire needs good men, Basil. I could think of no finer than you. I ask that you return to the City with me, so we might free it from this infernal bondage. Help me restore the liberty and freedom of the Roman people."

Basil's mind floated in a sea of troubles: the horrors he could not forget, the travesty his friend told him, and the iniquity in store for them all. And he laughed. It was devoid of joy, full of resignation.

Surprised by this false mirth, Dukas asked, "What is the matter, my friend? Has a foul humor overtaken you? Is your mind yet your own?"

Still chuckling, Basil rocked back on his stool and replied, "The Turk is at my front gate, and you ask me to crown you Emperor, is that it? HA! My starving army is glad we haven't been decimated, and you would have us overthrow not one, but two Emperors? Ha ha ha..." he trailed off.

"I brought an able commander with fresh mercenaries, Russians at that. He will not let the enemy pass. And I have Romans under arms awaiting my command, Basil, to help restore the Imperial Dignity.

And I will need good men like you for God to find favor in this enterprise."

Basil wearily coughed. "The Empire be damned, Alexius. Here I and a band of barbarians have bled to keep them safe, while they forget about us in a war they started. I'd rather fall to the Sultan's blade rather than accept the Pope's mitre, or be strangled by a eunuch in my sleep. Save that rotten world without me."

Dukas looked with sympathy at his friend's suffering. "This is why I ask you to return with me, my dear Basil: the good, true Romans have suffered too long for the Angelus. How many times have you bled without thanks from that wicked family? How many of your men have bled out in front of you while Isaac defiled the Crown with another dozen prostitutes in the throne room? I will end this, Basil; I will liberate the good people of the Empire from this oppression. And I will need a worthy Master of Arms by my side to restore the righteousness of the Empire."

Basil leaned back, color washing into his pallid face. "I know you to be a true man, Alexius, and I believe you would try your best. But with the Crown on even your head, the Court is rotten deep within. To win the powerful to your side, you will have to degenerate to be as they are, much given to pleasure and idle in work. Go with my blessing, but I cannot entrust the defense of my home to your Cretan."

Dukas moved to speak again for his case, but knew better. Hesitating, he turned without another word to leave the tent.

"Alexius, if you would," Basil called after him, as if in lost in the fog of dreams, "Could you take my love to Irene?"

Dukas turned, testily. "I would be glad to, Count Basil. I'm not sure she will be needing yours anymore." With that left hanging in the chill mountain air, the supplicant left the tent.

Constantinople, 18th December, 1203

"I'm sorry, my lady, he brought soldiers to force the gates!" squealed the sweating eunuch as he prostrated himself before Lady Irene. The sound of boots marching hard on marble echoed in the hall beyond the open door. Irene and John rose to meet this surprise.

"How dare you attack the dignity of my love!" exclaimed Count Basil, still clad in his grisly armor, as he stormed into the candle-lit parlor, flanked by a dozen Cuman warriors. Their barbarity contrasted with the delicately woven tapestries of nymphs and fawns frolicking in woodland glades in this inviolate place. Basil removed his gauntlet, shaking it at the usurping senator in a fury.

As his mouth began to challenge the Count, Irene charged, "And who is this tyrant who forces his way into my home?! With your mongrel thugs you dare insult MY dignity?!"

"YOUR dignity, my lady?" roared back the bearded warlord. "Your dignity? I go to defend all of Christendom, this pansy-boy senator fills my place in your bed, and you have the nerve to ask about your dignity?!" he finished, pointing his gauntleted fist at John.

"And what of it, Count Basil?" inquired Senator John. "You could have stayed here with Irene, if you truly wanted her. But you chose to accept a commission for glory and bloodshed. The lady deserves better than such a carnage-hungry lover."

"You worthless fop!" howled Basil, lunging to strike John with his mailed gauntlet.

Irene caught his hand in mid-swing. "Rage at me, if you must! I invited him here when you left. You tried to lie to me. You left me for your glorious campaign. You almost died on a frozen lake rather than lay in my arms," she spat at him, tears storming in her eyes.

Basil stopped, looking at her, eyes and mouth agape. Looking at her now, her wide, beseeching eyes, he was overwhelmed by guilt. Why had he cared what the worthless Alexius III had wanted of him? Why had he put his empire before his love? Slowly shaking his head, he spoke, "Irene, my heart –"

"Leave us, Count Basil," ordered Senator John, advancing to the warlord's face.

"Stay out of this, John," Irene quaked to her paramour. As he stepped back, she turned once more Basil. "My love," she whispered, walking with him, her delicate fingers alighting on his chest, "I have not given myself to him. But I know now you've never given yourself to me."

Basil's iron soul melted at the look in her eyes, and he protested quietly, "Irene, my love, how can you say that? You've meant everything to me these past years. How can you not know that?"

Irene fought to hold back the tears in her eyes, but one slipped out. She pursed her lips, but said, "I've thought about this for a long time. I spoke with good counsel, to see if I weren't crazy to think these things about you," she painfully chuckled. "But I know that it is true. I don't know where you belong, my love, but it is not here. Not with me."

Feeling her hot breath on his face, her hand moved to his mouth, her words in his mind, Basil understood what she said. Every time the Empire called, he answered. Never had he let another do what he thought his duty. Never had he said no, so he could stay with her. So that he could be there, for her.

"Irene," he began.

"Just go, Basil. Go fight your wars," she pled.

John placed his arm on her shoulder. Basil came to, pulling himself out of her eyes. He held back the tears, as he pulled away.

A grizzle-faced Cuman drew his dagger and advanced swiftly to gut the effeminate senator, but the Count stayed his hand. Barely whispering, the Count called the retreat, half-stumbling out of the parlor. He braced himself against the uncaring, white marble walls before his soldiers hurried him out.

His head was swimming. The torchlight in the hall formed a bright orange haze. He had done the wrong thing. He had bled enough for his country. One of the barbarians braced him. He didn't have to go to war again. He could have let another. He could have caressed her hair back, and looked into her eyes in their bed. The world beyond her walls he could forget. Let the Emperor fight for his Empire. He barely noticed his legs go out from underneath him.

John took her in his arms. She buried her face in his purple-trimmed robe.

She struggled to bury a lot of things.

Winter Solstice, 21st December, 1203

Isaac sat in the carriage, rolling roughly across the unpaved ground. He had ordered a non-descript carriage for this visit, so none would see him travel to this place. It was the darkest day of the year, and night had fallen before he arrived for the meeting. Between the walls traced out by Constantine the Great and those erected by the minister of Theodosius, there was plenty of land, some settled, some wild. His trip was into the wild.

He fidgeted with the gold-laced medallion that hung around his neck. He was alone in the carriage, and with his thoughts. He had consulted card-readers, astrologers, and oracles. He asked them, "Will I reign for long this time? Will I lose more than my eyes for this Throne? Will someone murder my son?"

Their answers had been all over the place, some damning him for bringing the Catholics here, some praising the angels that guarded him and the blessed purse he paid them with. Robbers and liars, all of them. But the questions did not go quietly. They demanded answers.

The holy father of the City, Patriarch John, most pious of the Christians in the East, had given him no comfort. The Crusaders demanded that Isaac place himself under the authority of the Pope and force his patriarch to kneel before Saint Peter's throne. Funny, Isaac had wondered aloud: what use had a man of God for vassals? Why was it so important for others to bow before him to find pleasure with God? When the Doge and de Villehardouin did not share the joke, Isaac knew every knee would bow.

So Isaac continued looking. His search struck on a promising possibility: between the walls of the City, it was said, there was an old crone who could see the unseen. The others had claimed that, too. But she spilt blood. That seemed more real to Isaac.

The rough trundling of the carriage drew to a halt, then slid back just before the coachman could brace it. The door opened, and the driver's soft hand took Isaac's, guiding him to his feet. Isaac asked to be dressed simply and traveled without his imperial diadem. As the old man was lowered to the hard earth, he felt and heard the crunch of the frozen grass beneath his slippers. It was terribly cold out; he could feel his breath take form as it left his mouth. The driver took the Emperor's arm in his and led him to their end.

"Turnips," thought Isaac. "I smell turnips." He understood some things grew in the harshest conditions.

"Who are you?" asked a withered, feminine voice. Isaac smelled no fire burning nearby. He could feel her draw her shawl closer.

"I am an old man with worry for the future. I hear you can see it. What is your price?" he asked, driving straight to the point. Isaac did not like sneaking around, especially to visit witches in the dark of night. Something about this place felt wrong.

He heard her shift. "I cannot see the future. Only he can do that. I see the present, and the past. I have nothing for you. Go now," she commanded.

It didn't register that Isaac should feel affronted by being ordered about by this filthy peasant. "Who is he then? I must speak to him. I need answers."

The old crone bristled imperiously, "He is not here yet."

The driver's arm trembled, but not from the cold, Isaac sensed. It must be something he beheld.

"When will he be here? I have good coin, so bring him now and it is yours," commanded Isaac, jingling the sackcloth purse at his hip.

The old woman walked over the frozen grass, away from Isaac, snapping twigs as she went. "There must be trees here," he thought. He heard a scuffle, and the alarm of a cockerel being taken against its will. The old woman's steps grew closer, snapping the twigs and crushing the grass beneath her feat.

"Dig here," she said, certainly pointing to a spot in the ground Isaac could not see.

Isaac patted the driver's arm, letting him get to the digging.

"Not him. You," the crone spat impertinently.

Very well. Isaac lowered himself to the ground, groping for the spot where he should turn the earth.

"Here," she said, stomping her foot where she desired. He crawled to the sound.

Isaac drew his knife from the jeweled scabbard and began stabbing the cold earth.

The cockerel struggled, flapping its wings and crowing in its struggle to escape.

173

He dug, for a half an hour. He loosened the soil with his blade, scooping the disturbed earth with his bare hands. His body shivered with cold, but he didn't have to see that which held his driver transfixed and silent. When he finished, he pushed himself back a small space, and uselessly looked up at the crone.

A rip and a pop came so quickly that Isaac did not have time to move before his insensate face was burned by the hot blood that spattered it. He could hear the hot blood filling the bleak hole he wrought, imagining the steam that would be coming off it. He heard his driver turn and run, his stomach rising in disgust. Isaac thought he heard something move after him, but he would soon forget about that. It may have flown or run, but certainly not slithered.

"Put your blood in it. Then he will tell you what you want to know."

"What?"

"Do it, or leave."

Isaac raised his knife to his forearm, cutting the back of it. It would bleed well, but it could be staunched well, too. He had played enough to find out the differences.

The dirty blade did its deed, and he trembled from the cold pressing on his frail body and from wont, as his warm blood flowed out. The crone grabbed his arm, pulling it forward to guide it. He gasped in suffering. The frozen ground was so cold and wet against his prone chest.

He began to black out. Then he saw something with his own eyes.

He was on a high wall, looking down. There was a lonely moon hanging in the sky, which seemed to shine more to show him how dark the night really was than to light the way. The sun was long gone, never to return. He felt like cursing the moon, but the moon did not make what he hated. It was all around him. He turned and saw a great golden gate, the Golden Gate of Triumph through which Emperors and generals of old marched in grand spectacles to show their glory and might, open wide, silent in the night.

An empty shadow walked back home.

Constantinople, 29th of January, 1204

The ceremonial guards of the Imperial Court stood impotently by under the towering stares of the Franks. This Court did not really belong to their Emperor Isaac, or his son Emperor Alexius IV. They only sat on the Throne because of the Doge and his Frankish knights. Already parts of the Empire had gone into revolt, refusing to serve the Catholic-installed usurpers or bow their souls to Rome.

The angered, blind Doge strode into the throne hall, shoving the heavy, gilded doors aside. Alexius IV startled in his throne, clutching his scepter closer. The shrinking courtiers parted to the porphyry walls, as the old man stormed down the crimson carpet, Count Geoffrey following behind him.

"Young Alexius," Dandolo seethed, "how long must we play this game? You owe us what you promised. Our patience is spent." He stood brazenly at the edge of the dais step. "Where is the money, Alexius?"

Alexius struggled to summon his resolve, his face twisting in scorn. The Doge imposed upon all around him, even emperors. "The coffers are slow in filling, so you must be more patient. And welcome to Our Court, honored Doge. We were attending important matters of state, which will benefit Venice, so if you will please leave Us right now –"

"I will do no such thing!" roared Dandolo. "Where is your father, boy? I tire of trifling with children. Send for him now!"

"I am Emperor here, Dandolo. Remember that," the eighteen year-old snarled back, the darkness of the night at his back.

"Then you will pay the price of your throne, or you will lose it!" the octogenarian scowled, taking the next step up to the throne.

The elite imperial guards unsheathed their swords, and the Franks drew theirs. The nobles of the court tried to melt into the walls, but the stone kept them trapped. The air felt solid, and silent, like a mold around those assembled.

"Where is your father?" growled the Doge.

"He is…busy," young Alexius struggled, attempting to put a nice turn of phrase to the debauchery his father had returned to indulging. "And he has no time for the likes of you," spat the young emperor.

Taking another step up the dais, Dandolo threatened, "My patience is done with you and your decrepit father. You will pay for the blood we shed for you, or we will take it from you."

Senator Sevastos and Nicetas Choniates, Master of the Imperial Academy, watched in wide-eyed horror. It was very possible that they would be murdered right here, this very night, for supporting the wrong side.

Finally screwing his back up, Alexius hoarsely cried, "Be gone from this court, Dandolo. Take your brigands with you. Already, I have ransacked my churches, melted down my altars, tarnished the faith of all my Empire, just to hand you a few measly coins, and it is still not enough for you! You will receive not one more coin from This Throne." The young man rose from his perch to stare directly into the white, blank orbs of the Doge. "There is abundant darkness beyond these walls; I give it to you freely. Test me again, and I will feed you so much it will devour you. Now go."

The old man listened to those around him: he could hear the fear trembling within every heart. Stepping back, he wheeled about to walk to the doors that he wrought wide-open. He will be back in this hall, but he will see it painted red.

The Senate Theater, under cover of darkness

The desperate men clutched together under the crystal dome of the Roman Senate. Alexius Dukas, backed by Count Basil, spoke boldly into the hush of the tense night. The men around him were the brave, the self-interested, and the powerful who saw this opportunity as their last.

"Fellow Romans, the last and only pillar holding the wretched Angelus on the throne is gone. The Crusaders have renounced their oaths of support to the August Throne and even now ravage Chalcedon on the other side of the Bosporus. I put it simply: you can hide under the banner of the Angelus family, shrinking behind these walls, praying that those who stand at the gates will not open them to the Crusaders, or you can join with me and cast down all those who would bring ruin to Caesar's Ghost. I will cast down the twin Devils from the Apostles Throne tonight," he paused, looking each man in the eye. "Now count yourself with Rome, or count yourself with Christ's nemesis."

Two of the six stepped forward immediately, pounding their fists to their breasts for the stiff-arm salute of the legions. The other four looked on one another, fear of this treasonous audacity in their eyes.

A tall, fair-haired senator spoke, alone."And what is the price of our friendship in this rebellion against the two emperors, Dukas? You becoming Alexius the Fifth will benefit you, yes, but what of us?"

Eyes cast to the hard, unyielding marble under his feet, Dukas walked toward the senator, placing a hand on his hesitant frame. "My dear senator, once the Apostles' Throne is mine and the Catholics driven off, there will be much good restored to the Empire of Caesar. Your share," he continued, locking eyes with the taller senator, "will be just and commensurate."

Basil quietly inserted himself into the circle.

The empty congress echoed with the dull strike driven into the senator's vitals. The proud man collapsed onto his face, his arms shaking against the silent marble. A boot lifted him from his tenuous moorings, dashing him against the rock. The others shifted their eyes from the punishment being dealt by the warlord in their midst, which reassured them to remain in their places.

Dukas steadied himself, his hardened boot having done its job well. "Does anyone else wish to ask what ill-gotten spoils can be theirs if they stand in the defense of the patrimony of Caesar and Christ?" He cast a jaundiced eye at the remainder.

"Hail Caesar," saluted one, followed, with varying degrees of enthusiasm, by the rest.

Dukas cocked his eye askance back to the bloodied senator, and Basil advanced, towering over the trembling man.

"Hail Caesar," he choked.

Blachernae Palace, midnight 4th of February, 1204

"Ah, the joys of wearing the purple," reflected Isaac. He had wondered, despaired even, if he could ever find joy again after his brother crammed a red-hot iron into his two blistering orbs until they popped like fetid sores. After such pain, such misery, can a man experience pleasure in what hollow life is left to him?

As the nubile young boy and girl licked at his flaccid penis, yes, he realized, he can. While the world of sight was lost to him, the incense intoxicated his mind more than ever, and the hands that played across his chest danced in a language he now knew. The moans of the concubines as his favorites penetrated them were a long chorus that spoke to his rotten soul.

"Your Majesty, the most potent elixir of Taugast is ready. The crushed unicorn horn will devastate all that your lust desires," came the Hindu's words, reverberating in his mind. He took the Emperor's hand, placing a delicately-wrought chalice of precious amber in the limp fingers. The harlot moved the brim to Isaac's lips, and the brackish honey began to ooze down his throat.

After he finished the elixir, it took a moment for Isaac to recognize that his penis was not being adored anymore, but the cries of panic let him know it had come. His new senses let him feel the terror of his debutantes as the soldiers came into the room.

"There he is," said Dukas in monotone.

Isaac hadn't expected this to be the one.

"Welcome, Alexius Dukas," said Isaac as two strong hands picked him up by his thin arms.

"Isaac Angelus, you are cast down by the will of God. No longer will you blight the Roman Empire and Christ's Church. Your reign as Satan's pawn is over," Dukas finished, sheathing his sword.

"So this is how it ends," Isaac considered. "This is how an Emperor ends."

Basil stepped forward with the silk chord. Emperor Alexius the Fifth stopped him. He took the chord for himself. A man only ascends when he claws his own way up.

Isaac felt the silk chord wrap around his neck. He felt a measure of hesitance. His murderer was scared, afraid he wouldn't strangle him right. How sweet.

As he looked down into the blackened sockets of the old man's face, Dukas hesitated a moment, but no longer. Tonight he killed two Emperors, Equals of the Apostles, God's Vice-Regents on Earth. With his own hands. The young man he stabbed to death. He didn't want to hear that piteous crying again. Not tonight.

He pulled the silk tight, and Isaac felt his throat crush. He had given up this life a long time ago, but his broken body hadn't. It tried to gasp for air, feeling a painful wet stop instead. His arms and legs tried to thrash, to gain any inch of relief as his lungs burned in suffocation. Mouth gasping for any breath, the people in the room watched the helpless old man struggle.

Alexius V finally relaxed, sweat on His Imperial Brow. He trembled as the soldiers dropped the dead emperor onto the purple marble.

The Asian shore of the Bosporus Strait, 15th of March, 1204

Emperor Alexius V Dukas and Count Basil spied the Catholic camp on the hill to the north. The Crusaders had moved inland from Chalcedon, seeking new Christian homes to pillage for sustenance. After murdering the father and the son, Alexius V cast out what Crusaders were within the City walls, barred the gates, and slipped past the Venetian blockade with an army bent on victory. This battle would not only further starve the Catholics, but it would also whet the Roman people's appetite for glory.

"Your Majesty, I believe the reports were right about their numbers. 3,000 soldiers under arms, 100 heavy cavalry. We have 1,000 more footmen than them, but I've heard their knights' charge is mighty as the rock smashing the seas," assessed Basil, leaning over in his saddle to whisper to the Emperor.

Dukas replied to his man, "It is good we have the advantage of them. With God on our side, we shall triumph. How do you feel about an assault this night?"

"We will be well-matched, Your Majesty. But we can affect their surrender or scatter them to the winds. We must bottle up their cavalry, though. Otherwise, they will rampage through our lines, and we will be scattered."

"Which is why I will personally command the cavalry. Basil, I entrust you with the infantry. I will tie up their horsemen in a direct attack, while you scatter their camp."

"Caesar, I would not trust our horsemen with Your Life. They are worthy against barbarians, but not here. I ask to use them to draw the Crusader knights away from the infantry battle. Isolated from the rest of their force, we can vanquish them piece by piece," countered Basil.

"Count Basil, we have twice their horsemen. We must defeat their strongest weapon with ours, strength against strength, to prove it can be done. I will lead them into battle. Fear not, Basil, for the Holy Mother rides with us," he said, signaling for his escort to uncover the prize in his possession.

What Basil saw was the Hodegetria, the portrait of Mary, Mother of God, made by Luke's own hands. The most prized possession of the Roman Empire, this plain woman, who loved and mourned her children, looked at Basil as if the angels stood with her. Basil breathlessly dismounted, kneeling in adoration of the woman.

"Emperor, this is surely a sign. Victory has always come with the Hold Mother's blessings. The City has always been protected by Her, and now She will save the Empire," he muttered dutifully. Basil had seen Mary's icon before, but never so close. Since his mother died of consumption, he felt a twinge of yearning for Mary's love; since his wife died bringing their son to the world, he wept for her forgiveness.

"It was the Will of God," dumbly mumbled the priests, who, by their inflection, only knew to say that because someone told them to say it. They knew not the will of God: they had never asked the first thing about it. Nicetas and his philosopher's words did better, but Basil always felt only she could heal these mortal wounds. Mother.

"As I said Basil, with God on our side," said Alexius V, interrupting the Count's reverie. A reassuring smile spread on his bearded face, as he finished, "We will know triumph this night."

"Let us ride, Caesar."

Basil and the footmen reached the edge of the Catholic camp's light before the alarm was raised, then he called the charge. His Balkan spearmen plunged deep, scattering the bodies of their fellow Christians on the fires that kept them warm. Resistance grew as they fought their way into the camp. Basil leapt into the fray; in his experience, the men fought more bravely when their commander risked his life with theirs.

Alexius V rode forth at the head of the horsemen, these being actual Romans, not barbarians on the dole. He would win this battle, with his own countrymen, with Mary's blessing. After this victory, he would return in triumph to the City and drive those bastard Papists into the sea. The Empire would have a true Emperor on the throne, and he would bring it back to greatness.

Crashing past the perimeter guards, Alexius slashed his scimitar through face after face, holding the reins and Mother Mary in his right hand. His countrymen followed behind him, moving past him, striking into the enemy ranks. Some were caught by prepared crossbow strikes, some hurled their spears into the heart of the enemy.

Basil knew this battle would be a sure test for Rome. The Crusaders and their footmen were well-versed in the art of violence in times of peace. Now, leagues from home, starving, and adrift in a sea of hate, these men had fear, shame, and faith to aid them.

The front lines crushed back towards him, a valiant Catholic rallying his daring countrymen to the defense of their last suppers.

Basil cried forth power to his men, shielding them from becoming mere mortals who would quit this nonsense to see their wives and homes again. The Romans marshaled, pushing back against these invaders who sought to destroy God's Kingdom.

Alexius V batted aside a lance with his Saracen blade, as he smote his assailant with the wrath of Heaven, cleaving the man from his life. The melee turned to chaos, his valiant Romans clutching Fate by its throat.

Basil and Alexius caught sight of the commander's tent, the enemy heart beating feverishly to protect itself.

Then the very sky trembled with the thunder of a thousand storms, the stained white cloaks of the Crusader knights rising like a mountain at the Roman horse's flank.

And then the wave was smashed by the rock.

Alexius felt the men being wrecked by the assault, their light horses pounded by the mighty beasts from the West, his men's armor flayed by the unstoppable lances of the Franks.

Five of his companions thwarted the line of assault to protect him, nearly impaled for their loyalty. "Caesar, we must withdraw!" shouted one with wild eyes.

"Rally the men to the eastern hillock! We will dash them again!" Alexius reposted. Turning to move to the sanctuary of the East, he was almost unseated by a friend, now ornamenting a spear, blunting it with his body to save his Caesar.

Shocked at the body of his companion falling in a broken heap past himself, Alexius recovered his senses as his horse burst in panic. Seizing the reins in both hands, Alexius bowed the animal to his will.

In struggling for control of his steed, he let slip the Hodegetria.

Mary slipped from his fingers, and fell to the muddy ground.

His life was pulled from danger in the nick of time by his man Josephus, who rode with the forsaken Emperor's reigns in his hands to the East.

Seeing their Emperor flee in darkness, the foot soldiers had enough time to question hope before the unstoppable cavalry dashed them with it.

Blachernae Palace, Constantinople, 16th of March, 1204

"Where is the Holy Mother?" demanded the Patriarch in his approach to the Emperor, who busy washing the defeat off his face in the palace.

Dukas dabbed at the soot, shame, and resolve on his face, the privacy of his bath chamber ruined.

The aged cleric, the spiritual father of the Orthodox faith, thrust, "Where is the Hodegetria? Where is Saint Luke's handiwork? Why have I had to come looking for it? In ages past, it was returned, in triumph, to the Hagia Sophia, Mother Church to the World. Why do I now see you skulking in this apartment without it?"

Alexius struck his fist into the porcelain basin, its delicately painted lilies splashed with his frustration. "Because I do not return in triumph, father, that is why." Turning to face down the unruly priest, "We were routed, and many good Christians died out there, while you were here, safe."

"And where is the Blessed Virgin, Alexius? You promised to protect Her!"

"She was knocked from my hand by a Papal lance, father, so I suspect she's lying in the mud right now. This Empire has enemies."

The Patriarch and his disciples recoiled in horror and shock, crossing themselves and shouting nonsense, like "God has abandoned us" and "the Virgin sees only wickedness in our hearts". As if they could not see that before now.

"The Holy Mother protected this City from the Persians, after they overran the Empire centuries ago! When the church fathers of old showed Her the camp of the enemy from the walls, the Arabs were scattered by her Grace, TWICE! Whenever we have needed Her, She has saved this City, GOD'S CITY, and His Empire! And YOU lost Her!" he shrieked, the rage boiling over in the Patriarch.

Alexius continued, hoping to end this inconvenient distraction, "There is no doubt they have it in their booty train, and we will not let one live after their surrender until they give it back. I will restore Her to Her rightful place, Father," he finished, iron in his voice.

The priest stepped back, mouth open in revulsion. "I knew you were ill-favored of Heaven. God did not favor you. You killed two of Christ's Apostles; their blood stains your soul…"

Having enough of the old man's words, Dukas stalked forward, "And YOU crowned me. Need I remind you, Father? If that is your game, you placed the Crown of the Caesars on Judas' brow, so you are even more damnable than this sinner! Now I have an Empire to save from your Brother's henchmen, so be gone!" he exploded with a flourish at the Holy Father.

The priest faltered back, trembling. One shaking finger accusing Alexius, "You will pay for this…" gasped out of the Patriarch's mouth.

Alexius chased the retinue from his chamber, slamming the amethyst door behind them.

He knew he would pay.

Constantinople, 12th of April, 1204

The night blazed with the agony of 1,000 suns. Great slings and arrows ended lives and shattered calamity in their wake. After the defeat of the imperial army in Asia, Dandolo and the Crusaders saw the arrival of the Holy Mother into their midst as a sure sign as ever could be of the righteousness of their cause. It's like finding a letter in your house telling you to keep going, signed "God."

The Venetian war galleys and the assembled knights of Christendom stormed the walls of the City, daring to be the first to claim it in the 800 years it stood against all the hordes and terrors of the East.

As the siege towers and assault parties discovered, even a coward can fight like a lion behind high enough walls. From the land and sea, the Crusaders fought valiantly, but to no avail.

The blind Doge studied the detailed reports of the walls. These walls had been built centuries ago by Constantine, the Great and the Saint. It had been reinforced by another the Great, Theodosius. They had never been stormed by land by any army.

"We will march by sea," he declared to the convened council of war.

The assemblage looked quizzical, confused by his assertion.

"We have ships mightier than their tricks; they have land walls mightier than our army. We will march our army on our ships across the sea and storm their walls where they never expected an army to march."

Count Geoffrey de Villehardouin, unhappy with all that had come to pass, could bear no more. "GENTLEMEN!" he burst out from his place at the back of the tent. "Does none of what we've done mean anything to your hearts?! We are here arguing the best way to bring another city of our fellow Christians to its knees! This is madness!"

Dandolo rolled his white eyes in frustration. "Really, Geoffrey, is this really something any of us care to hear about anymore? If you can't see out the door, we are already well under siege of this City, for the SECOND TIME. We've already overthrown one emperor and bested their army in the field. Your words are too late. Now sit down!"

"NO!" interjected de Villehardouin. "THIS IS MADNESS! You know very well that this is different than the first time. Then, we restored the rightful man to the throne and drove off a beast amongst men. Even then we plundered our fellows in faith unjustly. But you, you damned Venetians, you ordered the young Emperor to strip the gold and silver from the icons and his churches to pay this infernal debt you lord over us all!"

Dandolo growled as he marched through the crowd to stare down de Villehardouin. "A debt YOU orchestrated, young Geoffrey! Need I remind you, my people have put our lives and fortunes on hold for almost four years to support your foolhardy quest? If you had only been a man of your word and not the most wild delusions, the ruin of my people would not be at stake!"

"How dare you question my honor!" howled de Villehardouin. He raised a gauntlet to strike the old man, but he was set upon by three of his fellow knights. "We can settle that question like men, but this is still madness! How many innocents will die by Christian swords once we take those walls? What horrors will we visit on our brothers and sisters in Christ because of your usury?!"

The three men wrestled him into full submission, leaving his face alone exposed to the Doge.

Dandolo moved to speak in de Villehardouin's ear, saying, "Perhaps you should have thought about what you were about to unleash before you started this. Leave now if you want, but your debt will be paid, in gold, or in flesh."

Still uncertain about the tactics for the siege, one captain offered, "We have tried already to mount their walls from our ships, but they scatter us before we triumph. What new stratagem will you have us do, Doge?"

Grinning viciously, Dandolo turned away from de Villehardouin to explain, "Lash our ships together, two as one. This way, our weight will be unstoppable, and any attempt at retreat will be undone by the other. We will build great towers atop these pairings, as the sea walls are lower than the land walls and more easily overcome. We will send sorties from above the walls, and sorties will land and storm the small portals at the base of the walls used by fishers to collect their bread."

Another objected, "But Doge Dandolo, the sea is cruel and we will lose many in the landing. Perhaps we cannot sail closely enough to shore for this."

"THEN I WILL LEAD THE CHARGE MYSELF," thundered the old lion, the room crackling with his power. "I do not ask, I command! We have only the last assault before we are too consumed by hunger and failure to carry on this cause, which we all swore to see through."

Seizing the banner of St. Mark's Republic from a page's grip, "Build these towers and beach my flagship on the shore! I will lead the charge, and this old, blind man will show you thieves in the skins of men what honor and valor are all about!"

Save one, the captains and knights rose from their seats, shouting praise to Christ that this titan walked amongst men. The one regretted the effect this Devil's bargain would have on his soul.

The timid Greeks stood fast behind their wall, as the wall reverberated with the thud of the battering ram. This hall was small, and they were many, ready to defend it. Facing the sea, no cavalry charge could come through, so it was certain that they could hole up the damnable Catholics here.

A final thud blossomed into a roar as the bricks gave way, and a man plated as surely as a beetle struggled through the gap. The Greeks swarmed, pelting him with daggers and sword blows. He staggered back against the wall, stunned.

The Roman blades found no flesh, he realized. He stood up straight, claiming this ground, standing like a great colossus over the Greeks. They stepped back defensively, preparing. The man who wouldn't die came out swinging, and his companions poured into the breach.

Dukas howled commands at his soldiers, who no longer honored their descent from the Romans, to stay at their posts. From this section of the sea walls, he could direct the defense against the sea landings, still beating the Catholics back at many points, and direct soldiers to bar the Crusaders their advance through the gaps in the brick bought with many lives. He stood here alone.

"CAESAR!" hailed Count Basil from the steps below, as he leapt away from the boulder that shattered the battlement behind him. He was alight with fire's glow, from the assaulting ships and the City being put to the torch.

Recovering, Basil crawled up the steps to Dukas' side. "Caesar, we must fall back! The men have fled this section of wall. We can rally them at the Hagia Sophia. Abandon the walls for now, and make the enemy bleed in the streets. It's the only way!"

Alexius stared at the waters rippling between the giant war galleys beached on his shores. "There will be no rally."

Basil did not protest. He was still, staring in resignation at his friend, his Emperor.

"When word reached the rest that one gate had been breached, they all ran. The soldiers went, and the centurions went after them. I was wrong, Basil. I thought Rome only needed a strong leader, a just leader at the helm, and the people would rally. We could drive out these usurpers; we would drive back the Turks. We would make this world worthy of Christ's sacrifice."

Basil listened. He knew the cause was lost when even the Sacred Mother abandoned him. He would have poisoned himself then, just as Hannibal had done when all his sins had cornered him. But Alexius still held onto his promise, the only thing keeping him from drowning.

Alexius stood up straight, looking to his right, at his friend. "There is no strength left in the heart of men. They gave up long ago, my brother," he said, clasping Basil by the arm. "We were the fools who fought on."

A wistful smile playing him, the Emperor finished, "Get out of here, Basil. We can't save this world; it's already lost. Save whatever is still precious to you, and get out of this place." He embraced Basil, and walked away.

Basil stood there, the smell of smoke filling his nostrils. He had seen an emperor abandon his country before. He didn't know to condemn or praise Alexius for releasing him from his bondage. He had lost everything for this empire, everything that mattered anyway. He left his insides in the ice-choked mountains, which claimed Turk and Roman corpses alike. He watched the friends and strangers who followed him, as if he could bring them through the fire unscathed, be wholly consumed by darkness, wishing for the most insultingly base thing imaginable, just to say goodbye.

And while he was busy sacrificing himself for the Emperor's Pride, his love found another. One who wouldn't leave her. Alone. One who wouldn't die in a far country, where she can't weep over his body. He placed his duty to God and Empire above himself, and nobody else cared.

It was all for nothing. He looked out over the City, where all-consuming hellfire was being gorged. The people fled, or hid. In a city of one million people, ten thousand men who risked all would destroy the world. Basil did not find their audacity detestable; he found the lack of will in the Roman people disgusting. But they were timid. They didn't care. God always saved them before: why would they have to bother now?

In Bithynia, he had land and good men yet to count on; the Catholics could never wrest it from him. But land and gold do not fill a man's soul. Even Mary's love had left him.

Constantinople, the Night the World Ended

Basil braced himself against the vine-laced stones, his cloak crimson, singed by the flames through which he had passed. He looked up the stairs under the night sky. For some reason, the sky above was clear, even if the rest of the City was choked by smoke and ash.

While everything he died for wilted around him, he sought the one thing that had kept his life together. The woman that would never be his wife. If there was anything left for him in this world, he would find it at the top of these stairs.

Or at least his skull could find the cobblestones at the bottom of them.

He wouldn't say he was sorry: she wouldn't care about that. He would go to her and say, "I love you. I need you. Come home with me, where we will never be apart." She would respect that. It was forward, honest. Not open to doubt.

As he reached the landing, he doubted that he would find her behind these walls. Surely, Senator John had run away with her, using his money to save their skins, when he let others die in vain behind his feet. Or he, being a senator, may have just left her.

He pushed open the door, almost slipping to the floor. The water organ lay empty, its vitals spilled thence. The fires from the horizon penetrated the flimsy curtain, casting a purple light on the Count's face. Haggard and strong, he tried to remember the song the slave girl used to sing for them.

Basil couldn't recall the chorus. While it was written by a prince for his love, Basil knew it could say what he couldn't. His eyes fixed on the door, slightly ajar, across the parlor, leading to her bed chamber.

He slowly paced across the room, the ghost light playing on his face. Undoing his belt, he let his sword slip to the floor. He may have lived by the sword, but he would die without it.

His gauntlets struck the floor, useless, never to draw pain again. His bare hand pushed on the door, it yielding softly.

The reflecting flames let him go, brushed aside by the light of her chamber. Through the canopy of her bed, he could see her lying there, in one of her gold dresses. She thought she looked excessive in them; he thought she made the gold precious by her grace.

The slave girl's song continued in his mind, the words lost, but their meaning always with him.

He did not see the man's shirt draped near her vanity. He no longer cared for such petty things. His fingers brushed the soft petals on her dresser as he passed by, their testimony mute beside her beauty.

At the edge of the veil, he could see her beauty, he could see her face. He felt lost for words, but felt the music of their love moved her, too. His left hand being clean, it parted the gossamer veil between them, and the light that shone down on her grew brighter. He felt its warmth grow, and he sat beside her, lost in her cherished lips, slightly parted, as if for a kiss.

His right hand took her left, as he leaned forward, to make everything right. The ceiling bowed, the stones glowing bright as the sun, becoming their personal star.

Constantinople, 14th of April, Year of Our Lord 1204

"Unhand that maiden, sir knight!" shouted Nicetas, who, while unarmed, thought himself brave enough to foil the lusts of a man in full armor, wielding a blood-drenched sword that could cleave him in two.

Humility was never one of his strengths.

The French soldier was not one for words, and he didn't even understand the Latin Nicetas hurled at him. A mailed elbow to the Greek's soft beard spoke louder.

"Nicetas, let us go from here," begged his brother. "The City is lost, and we shan't be lost with it!" The pious gentleman pulled the dazed courtier away from the unfolding rape, unwilling to fight for that most precious thing when it's already lost.

Nicetas was dragged a few steps before he turned on his savior, pulling his arm free. "Run if you have no manhood left in you, brother! Run! There is no more shame I will bear this day," he spat angrily, as he went back to a fight he was certain to lose.

The Frenchman pulled back on her dark curls, so the filthy nothings he spoke could not be escaped by the young pretty. There was no fight left from her family for her: her father lay in his own blood, and her brothers ran away. Nicetas' hope for her lay in his words.

That, he discovered, was the best tactic after trying a fist to the back of the knight's helmet. The pain coursed through his hand as bare flesh struck forged metal, enhanced by the flat of the sword that soon flanked his face. The cobblestones greeted him on impact.

"My God," thought the courtier, "the swordsmen made it look so easy!" Watching their contests never educated him on the true strength of steel, or the hand that wields it. He thought it looked like such fun! Now he learned what skill the barbarians learned when they were not reading.

His vision cleared, and he could make out the Crusader pulling the maiden into the house, once hers, now lost to her forever. Another armed man followed after. Nicetas saw he was alone on the street, all the pillagers and refugees having moved on. Only the ever-creeping clouds of smoke were still to be found.

Pushing himself to his feet, the courtier had to enter a realm of violence armed only with wit and a glib tongue. He had lost everything these past three days: his closest friends gone, his home burnt, his ambitions wrecked. He could not let himself lose this. This young woman, though pretty, meant nothing to him: he had never met her; she obviously came from no worthy family. At this point, he only had the clothes on his back and a copy of the Republic.

He and his City had lost everything so far. But he would not lose her. Perhaps, his life. But not her.

Nicetas pushed the closing door back, as he stormed into the house after the Franks. "Stop right there, you scoundrels!" he berated them in Latin. They're Catholic: maybe they'll understand their own holy tongue.

The one shouldering the maiden had already made it to the next chamber, while his friend was still in the first room, small as it was, with Choniates. He stopped and slowly turned to face the Greek. His look showed clearly that running Nicetas through and dumping him in the gutter was an option.

Choniates was an expert in reading people, though, and he could clearly see that the knight was tired: all this killing and pillaging had surely made them weary. Wearing the opposition down with persistent annoyance was one of his strengths.

He advanced on him far closer than any other unarmed man would dare. He was going to make this work, damn them all to Hell!

"Now, you go in there and bring the girl to me. She is my slave, and I will ransom her from you." He didn't know where this was going, so he just grabbed onto the reins.

The knight surveyed Nicetas. He turned about and mumbled something to his comrade in the next room, calmly getting ready to rape his prey. Nicetas saw the soot and blood caked on their faces, perhaps seeing a measure of acceptance.

"How much?" garbled the shorter one in the room with Nicetas.

"Five talents of silver."

"Give it to us."

"I will take you to it, but first give me the girl."

The short man shouted into the other room, and the sound of tearing cloth came out of the chamber. A slap resounded.

Nicetas went for the door, but was blocked by the armor. "Give her to me, and NOW, or I give you nothing!" he said, jabbing a finger into the man's chest, anger showing in his defiant face.

The knight grabbed his left arm, bending it back at a brutal angle. He hammered a mailed fist into the courtier's soft stomach, making him contort in ways his untested body never had.

He was flung to the ground, the knight slowly pacing toward his coughing frame. Nicetas realized his bluff had been called. "Crawl," he thought. Crawl.

A hard-shod boot stomped onto Choniates' soft left hand, smashing it flat on the wood slat. His agonized cry was cut short by the swift kick to his stomach. The knights joined together to give freely of their vigor to their fellow Christian, with time not measurable by hours, but in repetitions to Nicetas' blackened mind.

The hard stone of the road snapped Nicetas to a semblance of awareness, as he found himself rolling on his side without a boot moving him. He lay alone in the street, his innards on fire, and the taste of copper in his mouth.

He heard her desperate scream, inside.

Nicetas lay on the ground, for how long he could not reckon. Her shrill cry inside brought him from his daze, and he remembered what he must do: save this woman. She might have been a harlot, or a woman who gives her favors too freely; she may not be virginal and unblemished. But she might be worthy of living, he dared, pushing himself off the dirty street.

All he knew for certain, of anything in this world, was that the Franks were robbing her, killing her, in their own careless way. They might be merciful and kill her when they're done using her up. Or they could leave her in her family's slaughterhouse, to be ravaged again by the next passerby. Maybe sell what's left of her to an Arab, so he can rape her with Allah's blessing.

Or Nicetas can shove a flaming torch into their pig-faces and watch them beg for mercy. Across the street, a house burned, devoured by the beast that will consume the whole City before it's sated. Running to it, Nicetas covered his face with a sleeve as he dashed for a flaming timber. "Oh," he noticed by the burning planks on the floor, "this had been a nice house!"

Seizing on a loose board, he bore it aloft as he returned to the crime. Possessed by a mad spirit, the Greek ran into the charnel house, brandishing the plank like a fiery sword. His eyes whirled around the flame to see a startled knight in mid-undress. Nicetas hurled his fury into a flaming broadside at the Frenchman's face, knocking him against the far wall.

The naked Crusader, his armor on the ground, barely had time to turn before the rampaging philosopher rammed the back of his head with the timber. He screamed as he fell, struggling with his nakedness and wooden inferno atop him. Nicetas grimaced in victory, and then took note of the maid. She yet held a bit of skirt in its place! He was not too late!

Nicetas grabbed the girl and took off running. The man and his maiden fair made it into the street. Her home became a hell behind them.

Nicetas fled into the street and was delivered by an iron fist straight to the stones below. The maiden got slightly further before the fresh violation of soldiers caught her.

The familiar boot caught him in the gut, followed by a stomp to his face.

His Socrates slipped out of his vest, which elicited the greed of one of the men-at-arms. Grabbing it up, the brigand thought it was a case for rare spices, or maybe gold jewels were secreted inside.

Just words, he saw. That he didn't understand. In a fit of rage, he tore apart the binding and the pages after it.

Nicetas rolled over in time to see the naked Crusader, charred and enraged, come out of the burning house, with death in his hand.

As Nicetas lay there, he got the urge to climb. He was surrounded, so it didn't make much sense. "But," he thought to himself, "it'll be better to meet my violent, horrific death if I'm at least trying." And anyway, at least it was daytime. As his friend Psellus put it, it always seemed to him so much more agreeable to meet your terrifying end when you can at least see it coming.

As his Republic was torn asunder, Nicetas' squirming body was lifted by his frayed, gray collar by another Frenchmen. The filthy cesspool drolled something at him in disgust, the universal language, and then pushed him to the waiting grip of two others. Nicetas realized that these men will be kind enough to keep me standing as this charred rapist guts me. How considerate: it just wouldn't do to slip on his own entrails.

One pulled the Greek's hair fiercely, allowing him to see the maiden soon to become the spoil of a baker's dozen of fiends instead of just two. He also saw a contemplative knight on horseback approaching, assessing the City, or what was left of it.

"SIR KNIGHT!" cried the courtier in Latin. "Please, sir knight, I am a noble of this court, and I beg your help! Don't let a nobleman die in such a miserable way!"

The knight lifted his visor, and raised a mailed hand to bid the vandals halt. To a man, they obeyed, much to the philosopher's ultimate surprise. He assessed his plaintiff and asked, "Who are you, good sir? I am Count Baldwin, of Flanders and Hainaut. What is this?"

"I am Nicetas Choniates, Chancellor to the August Throne, Lord of Chonae. My line is descended from Ulysses, as you know him. These men are attempting to rape my woman, and her virtue is very dear to me."

"Unhand him," commanded Baldwin, the soldiers standing down, as lesser beasts defer to the greater. "What is this woman to you? If my men desire her, and she is your property, I will compensate one of your stature for her."

Nicetas remembered: he didn't even know who she was. Baldwin had clear eyes and disciplined ears, so getting caught in a lie now would certainly be her ruin.

He had betrayed his best friends when it had mattered most. He sold one woman's love away from a man who had saved his brother's life. Why risk it all to save this one now?

The dark-eyed girl looked at Nicetas, wondering at him, glad for his heroism or stupidity. It didn't matter which, even if it didn't help.

Feeling her eyes move over him, Nicetas steeled himself for the truth.

"She's my sister. Count Baldwin, she is my sister, and as our father is no more, she is as my daughter. I cannot allow her to be violated by the likes of these, as a woman of noble spirit."

Not that this was the truth, but Nicetas had to get used to the idea first.

Baldwin eyed her appraisingly, weighing the Greek's words. Looking back to Choniates, he asked "And what is her name?"

Damn. Lies on top of lies. Nicetas had lied to somebody, his entire life. With this man, this god, sitting in judgment of her, he left it all behind.

Calmly walking towards the knight, he placed his bloodied hand in supplication on Baldwin's thigh. "Sire, I have spoken falsely, and I repent of it. I do not know this woman. But she is a woman, a Christian, and I will give you all I have if you let her free. Let your men satisfy their carnal hungers on me if they must, but spare her, please," he finished, tears in his eyes. They were real.

Baldwin listened and was quiet. Finally, his men standing in silent readiness, he spoke, "It is noble to sacrifice yourself for another, Choniates, especially with no gain for yourself. My men are granted the right to spoils for three days after a siege, and they will have their enjoyment of it," he paused. Looking Nicetas in the eye as the City burned around them, Baldwin continued, "But take your maiden and go. I ask nothing in return. Remember, it was your courage that saved you both." He uttered a command in their tongue, and the soldiers let them go.

Blood at the corner of his mouth, Nicetas hobbled past the soldiers to the silent girl. She stared at him, to which he only gave a curt nod, placing his arm around her. He had guided her only a few steps down the smoldering street when his strength gave out, pain and weakness overtaking his body.

She caught him, bracing him against her bedraggled body. She stopped his lolling head. He regained focus by trying to understand what she was saying, her lips becoming the epicenter of his mind. She eventually became whole once more.

Whole, is a good word. For people, it means unblemished, perhaps a blameless quality. "Her eyes," he thought, "oh, those were an empress' eyes!" She had thin lips, but a dash of rouge would do her wonders. Not that she ever afforded herself such trivialities, he suspected.

"Thank you," the words came on her shaken, sweet voice.

He smiled weakly, unsure of what to do next. He had her; now what?

It didn't matter to him that he didn't know her name. As he would later reflect, as his battered body mended, all that mattered was that she was alive, that she was still a part of this world. She was one person, maybe the only person, he could save from oblivion, where the kings and madmen all find meaninglessness in the empty silence. She lived and breathed, dreamed and believed. She felt and gave, shared and cried. There was and would always be suffering for her, but it was a life worth living. For his iniquity, for which he could only beg forgiveness from his unseen God, it was worth it all to him, just to save a life.

An Introduction to the World of Byzantium

As you know by now, <u>To Save A Life</u> is set in the Byzantine Empire in the year 1204 AD, when the 4th Crusade came smashing down on it, changing history forever. As I say in the introduction to the book, this story is historically accurate, but it was not intended as a history book, so to flesh out the world in which it takes place, I wanted to put together some background information for your edification.

First, what was the Empire of Byzantium?

Byzantium was the Christianized Roman Empire, a state that married the cultures of the Near East and the West, the imperial might of Rome with the Christianity. The Byzantines were a very spiritual and mystical people, who looked to omens and revelation as much as they looked to the sciences and philosophy they had preserved from the classical world. The Byzantines identified themselves as Romans as much as they did as Christians, because they saw those as one and the same thing: the Byzantine Empire was the universal Christian Empire, by right. The Emperor was the head of the Church.

Did I mention they LOVED to persecute the crap out of people? Once the Christian Church got wed to the Imperial Office, most of the Emperors and leaders of the Church saw any deviation from the defined orthodoxy as heresy, and they would launch wars, persecutions, and pogroms to purge the heresy. They did this because they believed that there was one God, and there was only one way to approach Him. Never mind that sometimes they changed their mind about what "orthodoxy" meant, but they were a passionately religious and philosophical people.

The Empire where all the action takes place in the book was not known as the Empire of Byzantium back in the day, nor until recently, when a French scholar coined the term "Byzantine". From the establishment of Constantinople as the capital of the Eastern Roman Empire 300s AD on, this Empire was known to itself and to outsiders as the Roman Empire. When the Western Roman Empire fell in the 400s AD to the barbarian onslaught, the Empire in the East continued to be known as the Roman Empire, with a Roman Emperor, and with people that referred to themselves as Romans. But in the modern world, we mostly know it as the Byzantine Empire, a reference to the title of the ancient city that Constantine built his new Constantinople on top of, which was a Greek city named Byzantium. Scholars use the different names interchangeably, so just go with the one that sounds more impressive at the time.

Second, what did it do in history?

The Byzantine Empire was both a part of and a survivor of the classical world that saw the rise of the city of Rome, its Empire, the conquest of the West, the flowering of Greco-Roman culture, the spread of Christianity, and the coming of the barbarian hordes. When the Western Roman Empire fell to pieces, France, Spain, Italy, Portugal, Hungary, England, and much of Germany fell into what is called the Dark Ages. While much has been done to dispel the idea of a "Dark Age" from history, let's check the facts: the roads and hinterlands became the roaming grounds of bandit hordes; the massive cities with sophisticated intellectual, cultural, and economic activity all went to Hell, some even disappearing under torch and sword;

and massive amounts of people were murdered, raped, and sold into slavery. That sounds pretty dark to me.

Byzantium lasted for 1,000 years after Rome fell, and Byzantium kept all that fun stuff we like to call "civilization" and "not being pillaged by a ravaging horde" going. They preserved the Greek classics which would later help the Renaissance happen, invented new masterworks of engineering and architecture which can be seen in the Church of Hagia Sophia (pronounced haya sofia), the al-Aqsa Mosque, and in palaces and worship sites throughout the Near East and Eastern Europe, and held back the hordes of Asia that would have subjugated a weakened, divided Europe before it had the strength to defend itself. While Charles Martel and the Conquistadors stopped the armies of Islam and turned back the tide in the West, Byzantium stood like a rock in the way of Islam in the East.

It returned learning and culture to the courts of Europe, and there is plenty of reason that almost every European monarch adopted a form of the name "Caesar" in emulation of the Heir to Caesar, the Emperor of Constantinople (the Germans had a

"Kaiser", several Slavic countries had "Tsars", Napoleon purposefully identified himself with the Caesars). Hell, they even gave us the fork. Who doesn't like forks?

Third, where did it go?

At its height, Byzantium ruled Italy (after a bloody reconquest), North Africa, southern Spain, Egypt, Syria, Israel, Jordan, Lebanon, Turkey, Armenia, Greece, Macedonia, Albania, Croatia, Serbia, Bulgaria, and chunks of Hungary and the Ukraine. It was really big. This also meant that they were stuck in constantly fighting wars on two fronts at the same time, and that is kind of a problem you don't want to have (just ask the Germans).

This is how things stood until the late 500s AD, when the Persian Shah decided to launch the war to end all wars, to settle the struggle for world supremacy with Rome that had lasted for 600 years. After a bitter struggle that lasted decades, the Emperor Heraclius (originally from Carthage, in North Africa) destroyed the Persian Empire. He installed a puppet shah, recaptured the True Cross from the Persians and returned it to Jerusalem, and went home, a wreck of a man.

Then the Muslim Arabs showed up. Over the next 100 years, they eliminated the ancient Persian Empire forever, conquered Iraq, Iran, and took from the Byzantines Israel, Syria, Lebanon, Egypt, North Africa, Spain, and almost Constantinople. It was an epic struggle for Byzantium to recover, and over the next 400 years, it was constant warfare for the Romans to reestablish firm control over Turkey and half of Syria. Under Emperor Basil II, the Bulgar-Slayer, the Empire reclaimed superpower status, being feared and respected by every country in the known world.

Few dared cross him, especially after they learned of how he earned his nickname: for 20 years, he ground the Bulgarian nationalist rebels into dust, and after the final battle of the war, he blinded 10,000 Bulgar men, leaving one for every ten with one eye, so he could see that way back to the Bulgar capital. When the Bulgar khan saw this ghoulish parade, he died of a stroke. Oh, and Bulgarians remember this guy TO THIS DAY. Ever want to see some Bulgarians get upset? Say something nice about Basil at a party.

Then Manzikert happened. After Basil II died, he was followed by a bunch of worthless imbeciles, who only succeeded in losing ground and bankrupting the richest empire in Europe. When a strong and worthy Emperor finally won the throne (Emperors frequently got their jobs because the previous Emperor got dead real good), it was too late for much to be done. After a major military loss at Manzikert in the east to the Muslim Turks (based in northern Syria), the Dukas family in Constantinople declared the Emperor deposed, put one of their own on the Throne, and plunged the Empire into 20 years of civil war. Because the Turkish sultan had made a peace treaty with the deposed Emperor and not this pretender, he declared the Empire fair-game, and let loose his hordes to colonize vast swathes of what is now modern-day, you guessed it: TURKEY.

While the Emperor Alexius Comnenus did put the Byzantine house in order, he needed military help. He was on good terms with the Pope (a rarity in Catholic-Orthodox relations) and asked for some mercenaries and gold to aid in his planned war against the Turks. He got the Crusades. Somewhere around

100,000 Catholics went rampaging across his Empire, starting fights, fires, and thefts on the way to recapture Jerusalem, which Alexius hadn't asked for. It was a mess: a big, stinking mess.

The Crusade did help to recapture some of Turkey from the Muslims, but then the Crusaders struck out on their own to conquer the Syrian coast and Jerusalem. Two more Crusades happened after that, both giving the Emperors massive problems, and then things went from okay to bad. The Comnenus family ruled the Empire for several generations, until they were overthrown by the angered masses in Constantinople, who installed Isaac II Angelus as Emperor. This was a bad idea.

Isaac had no real experience doing anything (his claim to fame was he hid from the last Comnenus Emperor in a church to escape being beaten), lost a bunch of border skirmishes with all his neighbors, and started on the task of spending all the Empire's money. In an act of familial charity, he paid the ransom to get his brother Alexius Angelus out of prison in Syria, who returned the favor by having Isaac overthrown while he was out on a hunting trip, blinded, and then thrown in prison. Isaac's son, also named Alexius, ran for his life to the Western courts, where he had relatives he tried to talk into helping him.

That was pretty much a bust. Until he convinced Doge of Venice Enrico Dandolo, the leader of the richest trading empire in the world, to direct the Fourth Crusade against the Byzantine Empire instead of the Muslims, restore his dad Isaac to the Imperial Throne, and get mad paid. Why did Dandolo think this was a good idea? One, Byzantium was weak at the time; two, it is alleged that he had been blinded in the anti-Venetian persecution that swept the Empire 20 years before; and three, the soldiers going on Crusade owed Venice a ridiculous amount of money that they couldn't pay, which if they didn't, would cause Venice to go bankrupt. In a merchant-ruled republic, that's a bad accomplishment for a leader to have.

As the story details, the Fourth Crusade went to Constantinople, restored Isaac to the throne, had a falling out with him, crushed the armies of the Byzantine nationalist Emperor Alexius Dukas, seized the City, and then went on a week-long rampage of burning, raping, and looting. Constantinople had been accumulating the riches of the East and West for almost 1,000 years, complete with holy relics like the Crown of Thorns, the burial shroud of Jesus, and the Holy Lance, and now a bunch of people who had almost all died in a shameful act (the Pope actually excommunicated the entire Crusade) got to take it for themselves. It was probably the single largest robbery in all history.

The Venetians and the Crusaders then parted up the Empire between themselves, thinking they were going to do things right where the Byzantines had been screwing it up all these years. To let you know how that worked out, 60 years later, the Byzantine nationalists completed the reconquest of the Empire from the Crusaders by capturing Constantinople, which forms the scene that opens the book. But it was a wrecked, bankrupt Empire they got back. It is a testament to the sheer determination and will to survive that the Empire continued to exist for another 200 years, beset as it was from both sides, by European powers who wanted to claim the mantle of Caesar for themselves, and by the Muslim Turks, who waged a relentless war to spread the dominion of Islam.

In 1453, the last Emperor died fighting the Ottoman Turks, who fielded the first canons to be used in warfare. Ironically, the Byzantines that fought to defend the capitol of an Empire that only consisted of a few scattered outposts did so alongside Venetians, Catholics, and Genoese, the very people that had once destroyed the Empire. The nations of Europe realized far too late what they had done in destroying Byzantium, the only thing that had been holding back the terror of Islam.

Yeah, Spain had fought a long war to drive the Muslims out of Iberia, but they were an isolated group. The Muslims of the east could call on the wealth and manpower of Egypt, Syria, Iran, Iraq, and elsewhere, and bear in mind, these were the richest parts of the world at this time (it would take centuries more of misrule for the Muslims to drive their economies into the ground). Several desperate Crusades were called to try to drive the Turk out of Europe as Byzantium clung on for its very existence, but these were too little and too late. By this time, the Ottomans had already begun the conquest of Eastern Europe, and would make it all the way to Vienna twice, where they were basically stopped by luck.

Fourth, why is Byzantium important today?

Byzantium and its fall left a legacy that still shapes the forces that drive the world today. Worried about global Islamic terrorism? Yeah, the Byzantines had tried, with quite a lot of success, to roll back the Muslim conquests and liberate the Christians that lived in those lands. So when you see news headlines of Christians and Jews being massacred in Iraq and Egypt, those were the people Byzantium struggled to save.

The Byzantines learned the lesson that in order to have peace with Islam, you must be able to defeat it. Muslim caliphs frequently made peace treaties with Byzantium and broke them as soon as they could, because their religion encourages them to do so (I didn't make it up, it's in their book). Heck, they're not even supposed to make treaties for longer than 10 years, because the jihad must continue. Oddly enough, the most peaceful times of Christian-Muslim relations were during the reign of Basil II, who several times smashed Muslim attempts to raid his lands, until they realized that he was not to be trifled with. He showed us that the only thing Muslim fanatics respect is power.

The Byzantine Empire has been outlived by the cultural commonwealth it created, and its ideas and inspirations continue to have tangible effects today. With the fall of the Empire, a Russian prince who had married a Byzantine princess declared himself Caesar. Until the Communist revolution, Russia and one-sixth of the world's land mass was ruled by a Caesar, and the Russians took that role seriously. They considered themselves the next Rome and tried to live up to it. However, Russia is a cruel land, and the resulting union was an empire driven by imperial majesty and inhuman brutality, a trait inherited from the Mongol khans that terrorized the Russians before they became free. Russian policy, even if nominally democratic, has returned to the imperial model.

In the Muslim world, the Ottoman sultan declared himself Caesar and comported himself as the Emperor of All the Romans, just as the Byzantines had done. This became a reanimated corpse of the Empire, full of a renewed strength that would see an almost complete restoration of its conquests, but this one built on rapacious slavery. It was a reborn Byzantine Empire, but with a Muslim, rather than Christian, soul. In modern Turkey, there is a very real effort being made to restore the Ottoman Empire and the Muslim Caliphate that the modern republic's founder Ataturk disbanded.

The key message Byzantium can give us is one of the importance of spiritual and cultural power. Europe is currently a culturally, spiritually, and morally hollowed-out husk, incapable of defending itself from its enemies or even a passive collapse. The citizens of Europe have little to fill their souls and dreams with, living as they are in their unsustainable, socialist utopias. They see no reason to strive for something better, they don't reproduce their declining populations, and they waste their lives away in frivolities rather than contribute to the human values of freedom, equality, and Christian morality that made their nations powerful in the first place. They also face demographic conquest by the Muslims they let into their countries, who will take away those forgotten values and replace them with Islamic ones, of slavery, subjugation, and the treatment of women and children as property, not people, just as they did in Byzantium.

The Byzantines were obsessed with meaning, truth, and faith. These are things we in the West must discover, unless we wish to join them in the dustbin of history.

For even more information about Byzantium, please visit langhornecreativegroup.com's Behind the Books page for recommendations on DVDs, books, and podcasts that will show you the rich history you've been missing out on.

About the author

Stephen Clements was born a poor, black child in the hills of west Tennessee, and he grew up in Memphis, where he graduated from the University of Memphis with his Bachelors and Masters degrees in political science. He then made another great life decision by joining the US Army, where he got to do exciting things, like hate life and see beautiful, sunny Baghdad for over a year. While there, his reporting on engineer missions for the stabilization of Iraq were carried by more than 17 news outlets.

Through a twist of metaphysics, Stephen is also Jeff Klitzner, who is available for parties and bar mitzvahs. He can usually be found haunting the Starbucks at Vanderbilt in Nashville, where he lives with a spiteful woman and two bitchy cats. He loves to travel, study history, and drink. Whatever you have will be fine.

Titles also available from Langhorne Creative Group

Experience the bizarre and tragic life story of author Jeff Klitzner. Why should you care? Because the most screwed up lives make for the best stories, and I'd put his up against any drugged-out rock-star you've heard about in the news. Go along for the wild ride of a man who went from a troubled childhood to qualifying to be a rabbi, to defeating the Irish in a drinking contest, and much more. You've got to read this book. How else will you find out how to get deported from New Zealand?

Welcome to down and dirty Memphis, Tennessee, home of some of the nastiest, most devious, and most violent people on the face of the planet. Experience nine tales of messed up true life, tales of the weird, and gang fights to prove once and for all who will rule this city of crack-heads and car-jackings! Written by four Memphians, prepare yourself for some raw and real pain dished out in celebration of the splendor and squalor of the City of Blues and Bar-B-Que.